One Man's Initiation: 1917

ONE MAN'S INITIATION: 1917

A Novel

by John Dos Passos

Authorized Edition, Complete and Unexpurgated
With a New Introduction by the Author and
Drawings from His Paris Sketchbook, 1918

Cornell University Press ♦ ITHACA, NEW YORK

Contents

Introduction, 1968

by JOHN DOS PASSOS

Sinbad was in bad in Tokio and Rome
In bad in Trinidad and twice as bad at home

Most of *One Man's Initiation* was scribbled down on the old French line steamer *Espagne* on the way back from Bordeaux to New York almost exactly fifty years ago. On the flyleaf of a new yellow notebook inaugurated *"at sea off the Gironde"* on August 12, 1918, I put down what lyrics I could remember of a popular ballad that had been running through my head as a sort of theme song all that spring.

Sinbad was in bad. He sure was. I had spent a most instructive year, first in the Norton Harjes Volunteer Ambulance Service back of Verdun and then in Northern Italy with the American Red Cross. The more I saw of that war, though I must admit I desperately enjoyed the travel and adventure after the dullness of four college years, the more I felt it was futile and senseless. I vented my righteous indignation in rather callow letters to friends back home and in Spain, with the result that the Italian censorship began to take an interest in what I wrote. I found myself in hot water with the Red Cross authorities when my term of enlistment expired in June. "Pacifist . . . proGerman," etc.

Like a good many young Americans today I had convinced myself that war was the greatest evil. Though not old enough to vote in 1916 I had been all for Woodrow Wilson: "He kept us out of war." His declaration of war against the Central Powers almost immediately after being sworn in for a second term in the spring of 1917 was a bitter disappointment. I hated the man for years after.

This is one case where hindsight agrees with youthful impatience: I still feel that Western civilization would have been less imperiled if, in spite of such provocations as the Zimmerman telegram and the torpedoings, Wilson, instead of sending an army, had used the threat of American entry to force a negotiated peace in the summer of 1917.

In my disillusionment I began listening seriously to the Socialists. Their song was that all that was needed to abolish war was to abolish capitalism. Turn the industrial plant over to the people who did the work and Man's aggressive instincts would be channeled into constructive efforts. By that time it was clear to every man of independent mind that the war was a senseless bloody massacre which served no purpose but to destroy the

delicate fabric of civilization. Why shouldn't the working people, who had everything to lose and nothing to gain from war and aggression, knit that fabric up again? We were young hotheads. We took to shouting all the warcries of the Socialist dogma.

In the end we were to discover, nearly all of us, that Marxism, hardened into a crusading quasi-religion, turned loose more brutal aggressions than the poor old capitalists ever dreamed of. In the summer of 1918, when, fresh from my bout with the censors and the Red Cross authorities, I dashed down my impressions of the French front the summer before, none of this was yet clear. At least it was not clear to me. The working class, in whose name the Communist Party in Russia was even then establishing its total despotism, still seemed the hope of the world. It's amusing to me today to note that in spite of my attitude as a volunteer proletarian, I used some funds that came to me from the sale of my mother's house in Washington to buy myself a first class ticket home. When you are in wrong with the authorities always travel first class. Through all the bluster I had retained a certain amount of worldly wisdom.

To tell the truth my motives were mixed. I shared this mixture of motives with most of my fellows of that college generation. We were full of righteous indignation but at the same time we were full of curiosity about the world at war. We had spent our boyhood in the afterglow of the peaceful nineteenth century. There

was a war on. What was war like? We wanted to see
with our own eyes. We flocked into the volunteer services. I respected the conscientious objectors, and occasionally felt I should take that course myself, but hell, I
wanted to see the show.

By a series of accidents some batches of letters and
scraps of diaries from that time have survived to this
day. It is a most curious experience for a man of seventy-
two to be confronted with the greenhorn enthusiasms of
his youth. Young people think they are so smart. Alas
the doctrines they spout with such fervor turn out to be
mostly parroted from their elders. What the young have
that is unique is an unjaded apparatus for registering experience; keen eyes, sharp ears, eager senses.

My first letters home were full of hurlyburly about
stringing up capitalist warmongers to the lampposts on
Fifth Avenue, but by the time I'd lived through a few
months of war, though I hardly admitted it to myself, I
had inwardly decided to let others storm the barricades.
My business was to tell the tale.

First I jotted down random notes in an old notebook
I'd used in Spain months before. After some ravings
about the beauty of the Catalan Gothic cathedral at
Tarragona and a sketch of some Roman arches, there's a
final note: "*Jan 14 .21—horrors.*" I had come of age.

Sailed June 20 1917 [I wrote in my first entry on a clean
new page]. Band playing hulahula on the wharf people

dancing in and out among the luggage. . . . La traversé—uniforms, smoking room crap games. . . . Singing. Champagne.

For we're bound for the Hamburg show
To see the elephant and the wild Kangaroo
And we'll all stick together
In fair and foul weather
For we're going to see the damn show through.[1]

That same day I wrote Arthur McComb, a friend from Harvard with whom I carried on a political argument which lasted a lifetime. I was always bubbling with enthusiasm about some new theory, but Arthur was a consistent reactionary. Even at that tender age, he admired Metternich more than any politician who ever lived.

A Bord le Chicago on a brazen hot afternoon, tied up "it may be for three years it may be forever" at the foot of fifteenth street NY. . . . I have a stateroom with three unknown parties and much luggage. The poor old *Chicago*, a typical one class boat, has quite the appearance of a transport, being laden with fear, patriotism and young men in uniform. . . .

. . . At the Socialist party's registration places—where people sign the petition to repeal the Conscription Act—twenty thousand have already signed in New York—that's in two days.

Courage!

---

[1] Quotations from my diaries and letters are given verbatim. Ellipses dots indicate omissions, brackets explanatory notes.

This sounds like an exhortation of St. Paul's when start-
ing out on one of his many voyages. . . . Alas when I fell
down before the Damascus Gate and felt the light dawn
and the Dove flutter at my throat and the taste of cocoa
in my mouth [this refers to the Liberal Pacifist newspapers
in England, then known as the Cocoa Press] I fear that I
too imbibed some of Saint Paul's less pleasing character-
istics . . . read my letters carefully as I may try to trans-
mit censorable news. Nagel—the name [of a mutual friend
who was an avid reader of Russian novels]—will stand for
chances of revolution and the psychological fringes thereof.

I've heard that things are very near the breaking point
in France. . . .[2]

Wartime Bordeaux was already familiar to me. I had
twice spent some days there on my way to Spain and
back. There I was too absorbed in the magnificence of
the seventeenth-century architecture, and the names of
the streets that echoed phrases out of Montesquieu, and
the smell of winecasks on the wharves to give much
thought to sociological problems.

Paris was all new:

> Night streets black
> No one out at all
> Cafe de la Paix
> > Remnant of Paris night life.

July 31st St Martin-les-Pres. Definitely I must start jot-
ting things down—

Paris: a strange Paris of whores and tragically sad widows.

[2] Letter of June 20, 1917, to Arthur McComb, in Library, American Academy of Arts and Letters, New York.

The abandon of complete misery. . . . I think in gar-
goyles. . . .

The men of the Middle Ages had the right idea in their
rollicking grotesque dance of Death. I want to write a novel
called the Dance of Death . . . but all my methods of
doing things in the past merely disgust me now . . .
damned inadequate—The stream of sensation flows by—I
suck it up like a sponge—my reactions are a constant
weathervane—a little whimsical impish—giggling—sneer-
ing at tragedy—Horror is so piled on horror that there can
be no more. . . .

. . . How damned ridiculous it all is, the long generations toiling—skimping, lashing themselves, screwing
higher and higher the tension of their minds, polishing
brighter and brighter the mirror of intelligence, to end in
this. . . .

My God what a time—All the cant and hypocrisy, all
the damnable survivals, all the vestiges of old truths now
putrid and false infect the air. . . . Hardy's Arch-Satirist
[I was thinking of *The Dynasts*] is more a bungling clown
than an astute and sinister humorist.

In Paris I met two college cronies, Bobby Hillyer and
Fred van den Arend. By an extraordinary stroke of luck
they were destined for the same Section 60 I was bound
for, assembling at Châlons-sur-Marne:

Bobby and Van and I had a delightful time in Chalons
. . . swimming in the Marne . . . finding things to eat
and drink, nosing about the rather unimpressive cathedral

and the lovely church of Notre Dame and the lovelier church of St Alpin—that has one of the loveliest square gothic towers I've ever seen over the crossing. . . .

. . . I'm sitting in the old beergarden of the erstwhile inn we are using as a barracks—in an arbor. . . . It is raining pleasantly and lucid pensive drops fall one by one from the smallish horsechestnut trees, falling with a faint kiss on the puddly gravel. . . . How ridiculous that Van and Bobby and I should be here! It's so very pleasant in the sloppy untidy garden with the Frenchmen preparing dinner in such a charmingly noisy manner and the children in dirty blue pinafores crunching about in wooden shoes. . . .

. . . The fellows on the section are frightfully decent— all young men are frightfully decent. If we only governed the world instead of the swagbellied old fogies in frock-coats that do. Oh what a goddamned mess they've made of organized society, the bankers and brokers and meatpackers and business men! Better any tyranny than theirs! Down with the middleaged. . . .

It is really comic to hear the young fifty years later echoing this same cry which I suppose has been repeated by every new generation since Man came out of the caves . . . and each generation has had to learn the grim lesson that the new can be worse than the old.

Even after we moved to the front I found time for moralizing:

August 2nd Erize-la-Petite. The damndest godforsaken-est hole I ever landed in. On the sacred way to Verdun. A small village straggling along two sides of the main road.

Most of the houses . . . have been very thoroughly destroyed in past bombardments. . . .

Complete dead quiet

Great concentration of ambulance sections . . .

Sombre broadly rolling country brownish tan with harvest—lowering under heavy rain and drizzling rain and mist and cat and dog rain—but always rain—

August 3rd

Rain rain rain—

Erize must have been a fairly unattractive town to begin with, but now, with half the houses mere shells full of rubble and muddy manure and the ground all about trampled to soup by crowds of troops and camion drivers —it is unbelievably gloomy—symbol of all the intense brooding boredom of war. . . .

. . . Walk in the rain with Van at night along the famous Verdun road—utter quiet—too quiet. This country behind the front has all the stillness of a charnel house, rather than the comfortable stillness of night. It is dark and damp and mouldy smelling like a tomb. . . .

But we are too near the front for any damn heroics thank God.

August 4 We are Americans—one realizes it. This is Saturday night and everybody is soused on the strong red army wine—nicknamed Pinard (bull piss) of which they dole us in seemingly limitless quantities. Of course rain and a foot of soupy mud round the cars. I'm lying in my cot set up on one of the stretchers in the car, listening to the rain and the rather pleasant sound of slightly drunken voices quarreling—I'm trying rather unsuccessfully to read Rimbaud's poems. . . .

Van and I took a walk over the hills in the rain through a harsh violet evening—crudely funereal—with jagged clouds in constant flow overhead. Tilted wooden crosses make every hill a Calvary. . . .

August 5th Have been shelling rotten beans—*Oh God Oh Montreal!* [3] We have to eat them tomorrow.

The great war novel is forming gradually in my mind. I have almost a feeling that the Streets at Night [4] will get encorporated—will be part I

Let's for the splendour of God have an outline!

1. Streets of Night
X and Y friendship
Miss Z—
The new Egoist—
From two points of view first serious Cantibridgian atmosphere—Europe motif—calling and recalling . . .
Death of X
Damnation of Z—alma
Part II The war . . . the philosophy of scorn
De trop de delicatesse
J'ai perdu la vie. . . .[5]

. . . I'm sitting under an appletree beside a delightful jade green brook. . . .

August 7th Again I'm sitting by the same jade green brook today an olive drab color because the drivers of the French section are bathing their Fiats in the ford above. It's

[3] From a poem by Samuel Butler which greatly amused my friends and me.
[4] Later published as "The Streets of Night."   [5] Verlaine.

a hazily sunny day. You might almost take the humming of an aeroplane motor overhead for the drone of bees in the tall purple spikes of some meadow flower that sways in the wind.

Bobby is assiduously sailing paper boats with almost Shelleyan enthusiasm.

Yesterday at this time my journalizing was destroyed by the arrival of an elderly gentleman with a fishing pole—a delightfully hale elderly gentleman with a sparkle in his eye—who turned out to be a natural philosopher and I am sure a disciple of Jean Jacques . . . he turned a stone over in the brook to show us the larvae of a certain skimming waterfly the which he used to catch trout with.

Strangely placid physical wellbeing—and enjoyment of the grass and trees and birds and the vast vague billowiness of clouds . . . alternate with almost frenzied despair at the stupid hopelessness of it all—a world enslaved to no end.

Apropos Van and Bobby and I, walking across the bald hills in the face of a great carmine sunset against which two aeroplanes darted and whirled in soaring loops—conceived a sudden plan, which sprang fullarmed and Minerva-like into the midst of us. . . . We are to return to America when we have served our terms and fight with pen and tooth and nail for free speech and general liberty—to try to make a splash, however small, in the stagnant puddle of the American mind.

Damn the police—damn the Cossack government, we'll cry and Junius papers, with a touch of La Libre Belgique will be a result—

August 7th (por la noche) I am sitting in my car watch-

ing the long luminous streams of the rain that pounds down all outside. Behind camions and camions, with their peculiar humming grating sound, pass incessantly—They are full of young men—gray camions full of gray men—through the luminous rain—the via sacra is noisy again—the holocaust with slow regular speed—goes past—grind of brakes— shush of wheels—an army corps is going by for an offensive . . . and we, infinitely bored, sit in our ambulances, waiting for orders to bring them back—when the offensive has been pulled off—c'est rigolo.

August 8. Today sitting by the little brook, opal and putty color from the washing of clothes above, we talked to the old gentleman, the natural philosopher (he had turned out to be the village schoolteacher)—the Germans had broken into his house and stolen his shirts and broken chairs in the fall of 1914. . . . Had we seen the broken camions being brought back? he asked. He hoped that there had not been a revolt of troops as at the time of the Aisne offensive. . . .

. . . And tonight sitting in his tiny garden on the road, looking through the little grille—we saw them—the troops of the first attacking regiment. He had just been telling us of how the villagers used to dance in the open square in summer—before the war—when the first camion—full of shouting drunken men—powdered with white dust—climbing about and dangling in all positions from the superstructure of the camion. . . . They came in long convoys filling the village street with rumble and shouting. . . .

. . . Then later when we were drinking white wine with

15

them and trying to bring the conversation back to its regular course—the commandant of the regiment—a delightful large man with large whiskers and round glasses—came bounding in with a little bearded captain with one arm in a sling and ugly long teeth—they were very cordial and pleasant and full of wonderful verve and animation—Theirs was the honor of attacking first.

August 10 I wrote Arthur McComb:

Stage setting: a small village behind the lines. A delicious pinewood whose gleaming needles brush softly the blue sky where wonderfully soft clouds skim across—on a hill overlooking a valley through which runs a very famous road—below, our little village—a collection of yellowish ruins—with all the green plots obstructed by motortrucks or by the regular ranks of the pale green ambulances of Section Sanitaire 60—

In the distance, above the sough of the pines is heard the grind of a camion clanking up the road—and the deep measured snoring of guns on the front. Way off to one side —in the direction of a town famous for its jam [Bar le Duc]—a battery must be taking potshots at German aeroplanes that are taking their afternoon spin, for you can hear a sound like someone tapping impatiently on a table with a pencil—

Personages:

Dos, seated on his haunches writing to an old goop of an Arthur McComb, from whom he has received no word since leaving Paris.

Bobby Hillyer—lying on his tummy among the pine needles—versifying.

Frederik van den Arend asleep in a little dell.

In toto a most idyllic scene.

— . . . I've built myself a snailshell of hysterical laughter . . . so far we have done nothing more strenuous than take our cars from place to place, holding them at the disposition of various army corps who don't want them or us —and invariably send us traveling again en convoi (twenty cars followed each the other like elephants marching into Barnum and Bailey's) down pleasant French roads to spend nights in pleasant villages.

Our major occupations are threefold—
    1 Searching for latrines
    2 Searching for omelettes and wines
    3 Searching for pleasant places in the fields and woods where to lie and read and write and sniff the dear soil of France.

France has manifold advantages over America; even in these distressful times. The omelettes are as varied as ever, though eggs are .25 apiece—and you hear no jibber about the glory of war: everybody is quite frank about things, amazingly so.

Of Nagel in France—remember what I told you—there are increasing indications. I'll tell about him in the next note.

I've come to firmly believe that the only thing that can save America is Nagelism there—King Alfred's patrimony [Great Britain] is the baleful deus ex and in machina of the whole bloody mess—as much as the Hun. Bobs and Van and I talk most excitedly of going home to Junius letters and that sort of thing—seriously and a outrance—Would you chuck reason to the winds and join us?

. . . Bobby and I are writing a novel [6]—doing alternate chapters and much amused—don't tell Cuthbert [an odd fish of a college friend]. I don't know why but I'm trying to cultivate a clamlike secretiveness. . . .

Van and I often talk of you and wish like the devil you were with us. Better hell among the pine woods than the shadow of the papier maché colossus.

August 15 there is an entry in the diary:

Tomorrow we go up to the Front to a devilish hot section. . . . Dont forget Athos, Porthos and d'Artagnan. . . .

Entries are scarce for the following week.

August 22 in a charming garden back of a little pink stucco house of which hardly a shell remains. It smells of box and white roses and is full of tall phlox blooms—I can't imagine a more charming place, though even here lingers a faint odor of poison gas. Three lovely brown and white striped snails hang on a honeysuckle branch overhead. If it weren't for the guns that bellow out around us every few minutes and for the occasional Boche shells—and for the sausage balloon that hangs with ridiculous gravity in the very blue sky overhead—one would forget the war.

---

[6] This novel, which between ourselves we laughingly referred to as the G.N. (great novel), kept Bobby and me busy and amused during our days off duty. Needless to say it was never finished. Martin Howe, one of the characters, appears as the lead in *One Man's Initiation*.

I feel too confused in the head and lazy to write anything yet—perhaps later I shall. . . .

. . . Curious how many shells can explode around one's very head without doing any damage. . . .

August 23 Things are quieting down so that I'm beginning to collect my scattered senses. I'm seated crosslegged in the dusty grove at P4; beside the dead house—a tarpaper cabin. . . .

. . . But I'm not there any more—I'm at P2, famous Hell's Half Acre while a merry bombardment goes on outside. Unfortunately it is too noisy to collect my pictures of the last week. In a way it has been rather good fun, in a way damnable. Probably it will be worse to look back on than it is in reality, though—the three big guns here are making such a racket that I really can't write. . . . C'est une sale de vie.

Note: the drunken camion drivers—"Il est venu mourir avec nous" Dance of drunken death. . . .

August 24 I'm back in our quiet garden. . . .

At present America is to me utter anathema. . . . I've been trying to read a copy of The New Republic that has come over and honestly I couldn't get through it. Its smug phraseology hiding utter meaninglessness—was nauseous. . . .

And far away the guns roar and fart and spit their venom and here I lie spitting my venom in my fashion. . . .

A bottle of white wine and a jar of gooseberry jam and an evil memory of canned goods on your stomach—such is war. . . .

. . . For some reason one falls back constantly on profanity. I've never in my life sworn so many swears or thought so many swears as since I've been "doing my bit" in France . . . and then of course when artillery trains get in the way and camions run amuk in gas-soaked valleys —there is nothing to do but swear.

August 26th Out of sheer desperation of laziness I have been trying to sleep—but as the flies and the fleas and the biting and nipping and crawling things that I have acquired in the postes de secours are equally desperate in their resolution to bite and itch. . . .

. . . The little doctor at PJ gauche bending interestedly over a piece of cheese "Mais il ya a des petites bêtes dedans— regardez donc les petites bêtes . . . qu'elles sont grandes." Meanwhile the shells fall, snort, snort all around, and the brancardier from the door of the abris shouts in vain for him to come in. . . .

. . . Also the doctor and the aumonier at PJ right— seated at dinner with the inimitable air of a function the blessed French give every meal, while shells burst all around and spray them with small stones, go on drinking from their petits verres, (conserved heaven knows how and looking utterly fantastic among the tin messkits)—continue with perfect calm to discuss some rather erudite subject, linguistics I think—

Later the delightful aumonier out looking for his glasses —without his helmet, chased by a brancardier who pops it on his head.

How wonderful they are, these nonchalant priests who wander about under shellfire, never a bit preachy, always

quiet and absentminded and mildly amused—They make things go marvelously smoothly and well. Imagine a troop of heroic American clergymen in their place. . . . The marvelous part of the French is how unheroic they are. The despair of them is absolutely Greek in its calm beauty. . . .

. . . Curious how impossible it is for me to write any verse—prose comes rather well but verse simply won't. . . . But gosh I want to be able to express, later, all of this, all the tragedy and hideous excitement of it. I've seen so very little. I must experience more of it and more—The grey crooked fingers of the dead, the dark look of dirty mangled bodies, their groans and joltings in the ambulances, the vast tomtom of the guns, the ripping tear shells make when they explode, the song of shells outgoing like vast woodcocks—their contented whirr as they near their mark—the twang of fragments like a harp broken in the air—and the rattle of stones and mud on your helmet. . . .

. . . It is curious to watch the effect of the performance on the section: some are scared green and are too terror-struck to think—others are seriously thinking—In myself I find the nervous reaction to be a curious hankering after danger that takes hold of me. When one shell comes I want another, nearer, nearer, I constantly feel the need of the drunken excitement of a good bombardment—I want to throw the dice at every turn with the old roisterer, Death. Death is God and pain is his partner.

. . . and all through it I feel more alive than ever before —I have never lived yet—You can still see the marks of the swaddling clothes—Tomorrow I shall live to the dregs or

today I shall die. It's much the same in the end—How
damned ridiculous!

That, except for a few scraps of ill-formed verse is all
there is in that notebook. The next one got lost. August
27 I'm writing Arthur McComb again: [7]

Van and I were sitting side by side in a pitiful forsaken
garden we spend our hours off duty in, and he was just
opening your letter when a shell shrieked over our heads
and exploded with a vicious pang! on the hill behind us. Of
one voice we cried "How ridiculous." Isn't it damned absurd that one of your serene epistles, redolent of eighteenth
century abbés peeing in their gardens after their morning
cup of chocolate and thinking sonorous cadences of liberty
and the world enlightened should be opened to the accom-
paniment of a bursting shell. . . . Oh Arthur can't we do
something, we who still have eyes in our heads and thoughts
in our minds? Can't we stop this wailing over the dead? Our
life is a wake over the corpse of an elaborately garbed
liberty that I suspect was purely mythical anyway. Like
the Jews at their wailing place the Liberals cover their
heads with their robes of integrity and wail, wail, wail—
God I'm tired of wailing. I want to assassinate.

The joy of being at the front is that one is away from the
hubbub of tongues, from the miasma of lies that is suffocat-
ing the world like the waves of poison gas the French and
Germans reciprocally honor each other with. Then too the

[7] Letter in Library, American Academy of Arts and Letters,
New York.

excitement is splendid, for us, to whom it is new, but it will soon wear off, however, into the utterist routine.

"Pensez," said a stifled muledriver who lurched into a dugout we were lying in during a gas attack one night "Qu'il y a des gens qui boivent le café sur les boulevards.". . .

. . . I shall never forget the frightened eyes of the horses —choking of gas standing beside their overturned guncarriages waiting for the shell that will finish them. And the drunken troops we saw go by . . . while the old schoolmaster kept saying "Il n'etait pas comme ca en dix neuf cent seize. Il y avait de la discipline." And his charming wife, hugging a kitten closer to her, her black eyes full of tears, answering: "Mais mon cher que voulez vous? Les pauvres petits, ils savent qu'il vont a la mort."

By early September we were *en repos*. No casualties. One case of shell shock. Shell fragments through several ambulances. One of them chewed up my cap I'd left on the seat of the car when I dove into a shelter. Looked like rats had been at it. A good deal of vomiting and diarrhea but no real case of gas poisoning.

September 12 I was writing Arthur from a small village in the Argonne.[8] The volunteer ambulance services were being taken over by the American Red Cross, preparatory to being absorbed into the U.S. Army. Most of us hated the prospect. Later when I actually served in the Medical Corps, I realized how silly I'd

[8] Letter in Library, American Academy of Arts and Letters, New York.

been. It was in the army I first got to know the great mass of my fellow citizens. Looking back on it now it was the most valuable part of my wartime initiation.

Sept 12
Remicourt

Arthur,

The Government has us in its clutches—picture the scene: An automobile full of gentlemen with large jowls in U.S. Army uniforms—Richard Norton [9] courtly in a monacle . . . in front a large crowd of ambulance drivers —behind them a much shrapnel-holed barnlike structure, our cantonment—the section dog by name P2 wanders about uneasily. An occasional shell screeches overhead, makes the fatjowled gentlemen duck and blink and crashes on the riverbank opposite, making much dust fly but causing no apparent damage. Mr. Norton has just finished his very modest speech ending with the wonderful phrase "As gentlemen volunteers you enlisted in this service and as gentlemen volunteers I bid you farewell."

What a wonderful phrase "gentlemen volunteers," particularly if punctuated as it was by a shell bursting thirty feet away which made everyone clap on their tin helmets and crouch like scared puppies under a shower of pebbles and dust. Thereupon, to be truthful, the fat-jowled gentlemen lost their restraint and their expression of tense interest

[9] Dick Norton, aesthete, indomitable archaeologist, the man who smuggled half the Ludovici throne out of Italy, a Harvard man of the old nineteenth-century school, snob if you like, but solid granite underneath.

25

(like that which is often seen in people about to be seasick) and bolted for the abris.

But all this is merely to announce that I have sworn solemn vows to remain for the rest of my days a gentleman volunteer—

Let us all be gentlemen volunteers in life and rollick through it mindless of the insane gibberish talked about us, of the musket barrels they threaten us with—.

Doesn't the phrase make you think of the bands of gentlemen-volunteers, gentlemen-adventurers who swaggered over to the continent in the time of Elizabeth to fight for liberty and conscience in the Netherlands—They drank and roistered and whored their way through the wars to the consternation of their allies and to the great edification of posterity—We of the Norton Harjes ambulance are much like that—we refuse the yoke and it is rumored and hoped that a new organization is to be formed in Italy to carry wounded across the Alps and through the Lakes! [10]

We are en repos at a village named Remicourt where they make the most delicious cheeses mortal ever ate— Camembert by creed, but young and chaste and tender and reeking with an ozone of clover and cows and placid contemplation. Van and I, apart from a few trifling military duties, such as trying to induce the very lazy French mechanics to repair our cars—spend all our time sitting under a haystack reading and contemplating and eating the aforementioned cheeses through Elysian September days "season of mists and mellow fruitfulness." In the evening we go to a

[10] At the bottom of the page there's a drawing of stickmen operating a gondola with a red cross on it.

café in the next town and drink infinities of café-au-lait or white wine with syrop de groseille—while poilus around us sing and mutter revolt and shrug their shoulders and say 'on les aura' (according to their mental complexion) and we are all very angry and hurt and surprised when at 8:30, by military law, the café closes and turns us out into the starlight. Then we wander home and watch the reflections of star-shells on the front beyond the horizon and hear the guns popping at a Boche avion that's bombarding a certain unfortunate railway station behind us.

. . . Wartime France is very much pleasanter than peacetime America. I am torn between a desire to 'eave 'arf a brick into the middle of things over there, and to penetrate a little deeper into the tragic farce that has projected them. . . .

Amateur proletarian or gentleman volunteer? Young people love to act a part but I could never quite decide which character I was playing. Well, quite a gang of us enlisted in the Red Cross for Italy. The Powers that Were felt Italian morale, shaky after Caporetto, might be stiffened by the sight of some fresh American faces. After a series of adventures which seemed to us extremely comic we reached the Italian front. We enjoyed the scenery. We reveled in painting and architecture. We did the best we could trundling the wounded and the frostbite and pneumonia cases down the mountain roads to the hospitals in the valley of the Brenta, but when we began to complain in letters home of the war generally and particularly of how the Italian officers treated their men the censors took a dim view.

In July 1918 I wrote Arthur from Paris: [11]

I am trying to get the Red Cross to swallow its words and its dishonorable discharge all of which were based on nothing but rumor. The extreme lack of decency, of small obvious humanness in people comes out more every day. They are preposterous. I refuse to take them seriously.

I want to retire to a valley among high mountains.— Shelley's Caucasus will do—and there live among paintpots and white paper and work in a vineyard for a farthing a day. Je suis desenchanté. If monasteries were the thing nowadays I should have been in one long ago. Let's found one at the end of Finisterre.

. . . Maybe I'll try the American ambulance service and be ditched forever but my eyes are so bad I doubt if I should be accepted.

A month later I was on the *Espagne* on my way home, writing my head off and determined to get into the U.S. Army at any cost. An erstwhile college friend serving in Intelligence told me I'd never be allowed in the AEF and I was bound I'd prove him a liar.

In my new yellow notebook I picked up my diary again.

August 12 just finished the Duchess of Malfi and The White Devil . . . wonderfully expressive of the swarming

[11] Letter in Library, American Academy of Arts and Letters, New York.

festering life of Italian courts in the Renaissance and the English of them is as superb as anything I've ever seen, firmer and less winsome than Shakespeare's garrulous style, more calculated. . . . August 13 Reading the 'Confessions' of Jean-Jacques—awfully good fun. How amusing that . . . what? I am terribly distrait today—I keep sinking into the blissful coma I always get into at sea. . . . Must reread those Webster plays. . . . What I meant to say about the Confessions was that Jean-Jacques has a morbidly deft way of bringing to the fore and deploring all the disgusting little nastinesses that so sicken one in oneself—all the puny lack of generosity, of frankness, of honesty that keep cropping up even in one who doesn't care enough about what happens to him to trouble to be consciously small. . . . We have left the little cruiser and the two gaily camouflaged ships of our convoy and are going off on our own about S.W. with a fair blue sea and a pale sky and a few white-caps to starboard. . . . August 16. I think I am right in my estimate of the point of view of intellectual Americans as to pulling the world by the nose via propaganda—There is a forceful malignity about their attitude that surprises and delights me—an intoxication with power that will have great consequences. It is as far different from the flabby benevolence Americans have pretended to as is German megalomania is from their old sentimental "idealistic" placidity. I wonder though if the piratic energy the war has generated in America won't have interesting results. Quien sabe?

Am getting along really famously [with *One Man's Initiation*] as far as quantity goes. God can take care of the quality:

There was a delegation of Greek priests aboard led by the Metropolitan of Athens—"many black spade beards and fine large Greek noses."

August 17 Awfully funny. While I write a YMCA man is being questioned by the interpreter of the Papa Greco about the origins and intentions of the YMCA . . . have been reading the fifth book of Divi Rabelais and have been stuffing with food all day until I am like a larded fowl. . . .

The scorn in the damn YMCA man's voice while he talks to the bearded papas is rather disgusting. I wonder whether the verminous subtilizing of the east is not humaner than the smug moralities of the YMCA. I wish I could find a drop of charity in my soul for these people. They are sincere and wellmeaning I suppose, but Oh God . . . if there had been no Lucretius, no Montaigne, no Rabelais, no Villon, what a dreary world!

Next day, the 18th, was a Sunday:

. . . Hurrah for the inapt—what did I do today but attend the Protestant service, the hymndroning and the brutal energy-worshipping sermon and the badly played Largo and all, and the prayer for the Allies and the thanking of God for his efforts in deflecting submarines from the good ship *Espagne* and then to cap the climax I passed the plate. I passed the plate! . . .

Alas the emotional stress was such that I've been unable to work all day—and I've had to feed myself huge chapters of Rabelais to keep from dissolving in tears of holiness. . . . But I have only two days and a half to write three whole sections and to end Part IV. Dépêchons nous. Whatever happens I've passed the plate.

August 19 Ruthful ruminatings over my disasters etc. to the tune of the Memoires of Jean-Jacques. At all costs I will not stay still. The flesh today is of a weakness indescribable. . . .

Notes for Pt IV #6
 The troops passing
 Ennui
 D.J.
 Road under Bombardment
 The Dugout beside the cemetery
 The officers' boots
 The donkeys—the road the morning after gas
 The soup kitchen
 The man who danced Spanish fashion
 The beginning barrage
 The broken stretcher
  in the dugout
 Lunch in the dugout
 the shells nearer and nearer
 The gas—the man's voice shrieking
  The men who drank guiolle
 The padre and the doctor dine
  Dampierre le chateau

The conversation
The second attack

August 20th Sea and sky splendid—blue sea and blue sky with softest clouds. I have fallen into a nasty frittering humor in which it is terribly difficult for me to do anything. The great novel languishes. I am filled with desire for curious distant places and for drawing. My eyes feel rather feeble and I am generally overfed, overdrunk, everything. Lack of exercise, etc. make me feel like the people in Rabelais who slashed themselves to let the fat show through their skin—like the silk in slashed hose and, instead of dying, burst.

Instead of finishing the narrative I seem to have spent my time until we reached the Narrows trying to work up a poem, which reads pretty trashy at this late date, called "Figaro Sings in the Steerage." The refrain ran:

> *Grey riverbanks in the dusk*
> *Melting away into mist*
> *And a shrill wind harsh off the sea.*
> *O the voices of sailors singing.*

I seem to have finished the novel in New York while I was resorting to all sorts of finaglings to get myself into the army and back overseas. I have no recollection of where I had it typed or whether I carried it with me in my rucksack when I sailed out of New York harbor with the Medical Corps ambulance on the troopship *Cedric*. I certainly had it with me when, the spring after the Armistice, I turned up in Paris with the Sorbonne detachment. "Trilby" Ewer of the London *Daily Herald* introduced me to Allen and Unwin, very respectable English publishers. I was in Spain, on a rather flimsy assignment for his newspaper when the English publisher wrote me that they would publish it if I would pay part of the costs. Somehow I scraped up two or three hundred dollars. Then they wrote that the printer refused to print the swearwords and various conversations which he considered indecent. After some soulsearching I decided half a loaf was better than no bread and wrote Allen and Unwin to let the printer bowdlerize what he would. The book was hardly a success. After six months I was sent a statement of sales: 63 copies.

After the publication of *Three Soldiers* George Doran imported a few sheets to America. Later the Philosophical Library reprinted a small edition under the title *First Encounter*.

And now half a century later the original uncorrected page proofs turn up in the Cornell University Library. Hence this new edition, which, for better or worse, presents the book as it was originally written.

Spence's Point
Westmoreland, Va.
May 27, 1968

Preface, 1945*

I T just happens that I'm looking over this little book
with a view to its publication at a time when I'm in
the middle of writing up the notes of another tour to another front in another war. This narrative was written
more than a quarter of a century ago by a bookish
young man of twenty-two who had emerged half-baked
from Harvard College and was continuing his education
driving an ambulance behind the front in France. The
young man who wrote it was about the same age as so
many of the young men I was seeing and talking to last
winter in the Pacific. All the time I was trying to imagine how I'd be thinking and feeling if I were that young
man again, really in the war up to my ears, instead of
being a middle-aged literary man getting a couple of
quick looks at it as a correspondent.

* *One Man's Initiation: 1917* was reprinted by the Philosophical
Library in 1945 under the title *First Encounter*. This preface—
called "A Preface Twenty-Five Years Later"—originally appeared
in that edition of the novel. Mr. Dos Passos took the title *First
Encounter* from a beach of the same name on Cape Cod—
PUBLISHER.

There would be a number of differences.

For one thing I think the brutalities of war and oppression came as less of a shock to people who grew up in the thirties than they did to Americans of my generation, raised as we were during the quiet afterglow of the nineteenth century, among comfortably situated people who were confident that industrial progress meant an improved civilization, more of the good things of life all around, more freedom, a more humane and peaceful society. To us, the European war of 1914–1918 seemed a horrible monstrosity, something outside of the normal order of things like an epidemic of yellow fever in some place where yellow fever had never been heard of before.

The boys who are fighting these present wars got their first ideas of the world during the depression years. From the time they first read the newspapers they drank in the brutalities of European politics with their breakfast coffee.

War and oppression in the early years of this century appeared to us like stinking slums in a city that was otherwise beautiful and good to live in, blemishes that skill and courage would remove. To the young men of today these things are inherent deformities of mankind. If you have your club foot you learn to live with your club foot. That doesn't mean they like the dust and the mud and the fatigue and the agony of war or the oppression of man by man any better than we did. But the ideas of these things are more familiar.

Looking back it is frightening to remember that naive ignorance of men and their behavior through history which enabled us to believe that a revolution which would throw the rascals out of the saddle would automatically, by some divine order of historical necessity, put in their places a band of benign philosophers. It was only later that some of us came to understand that when you threw out King Log you were like as not to get King Stork in his place.

Nobody had given a thought to educating us in the traditional processes of self-government or in the rule that individual liberty, wherever it has existed in the world, has come as the result of a balance between the rights and duties of various contending individuals or groups, every man standing up for himself within the framework of a body of laws and customs. Having no knowledge of the society we had grown up in, or of the traditional attitudes that had produced in us the very ethical bent which made war and tyranny abhorrent to us, we easily fell prey to the notion that by a series of revolutions like the Russian the working people of the world could invent out of their own heads a reign of peace and justice. It was an illusion like the quaint illusion the early Christians had that the world would come to an end in the Year One Thousand.

37

In reporting a conversation we had with a congenial bunch of Frenchmen one night in a little town where the division was *en repos,* I tried to get some of this down on paper. As an American unaccustomed to the carefully articulated systems of thought which in those days were still part of the heritage of the European mind, I remember being amazed and delighted to meet men who could formulate their moral attitudes, Catholic, Anarchist, Communist, so elegantly. Reading it over I find the chapter scrappy and unsatisfactory, but I am letting it stand because it still expresses, in the language of the time, some of the enthusiasms and some of the hopes of young men already marked for slaughter in that year of enthusiasms and hopes beyond other years, the year of the October Revolution.

It was this sanguine feeling that the future was a blank page to write on, focusing first about the speeches of Woodrow Wilson and then about the figure of Lenin, that made the end of the last war so different from the period we are now entering. Perhaps the disillusionments of the last quarter of a century have taught us that there are no short cuts to a decent ordering of human affairs, that the climb back up out of the pit of savagery to a society of even approximate justice and freedom must necessarily be hard and slow. We can only manage one small step at a time. The quality of the means we use will always determine the ends we reach.

Last winter, talking to the young men out in the

Pacific I found that most of them just hoped that what they would return to after the war would not be worse than what they had left. This is not an age of illusions. We can only hope that it will become an age of clear thinking.

JOHN DOS PASSOS

Provincetown, Mass.
April 26, 1945

One Man's Initiation: 1917

A NOVEL BY JOHN DOS PASSOS

To the memory of those with whom I saw rockets in the sky, on the road between Erize-la-Petite and Erize-la-Grande, in that early August twilight in the summer of 1917.

Chapter I

In the huge shed of the wharf, piled with crates and baggage, broken by gang-planks leading up to ships on either side, a band plays a tinselly Hawaiian tune; people are dancing in and out among the piles of trunks and boxes. There is a scattering of khaki uniforms, and many young men stand in groups laughing and talking in voices pitched shrill with excitement. In the brown light of the wharf, full of rows of yellow crates and barrels and sacks, full of racket of cranes, among which winds in and out the trivial lilt of the Hawaiian tune, there is a flutter of gay dresses and coloured hats of women, and white handkerchiefs.

The booming reverberation of the ship's whistle drowns all other sound.

After it the noise of farewells rises shrill. White handkerchiefs are agitated in the brown light of the shed. Ropes crack in pulleys as the gang-planks are raised.

Again, at the pierhead, white handkerchiefs and cheering and a flutter of coloured dresses. On the wharf building a flag spreads exultingly against the azure afternoon sky.

Rosy yellow and drab purple, the buildings of New York slide together into a pyramid above brown smudges of smoke standing out in the water, linked to the land by the dark curves of the bridges.

In the fresh harbour wind comes now and then a salt-wafting breath off the sea.

Martin Howe stands in the stern that trembles with the vibrating push of the screw. A boy standing beside him turns and asks in a tremulous voice, "This your first time across?"

"Yes. . . . Yours?"

"Yes. . . . I never used to think that at nineteen I'd be crossing the Atlantic to go to a war in France." The boy caught himself up suddenly and blushed. Then swallowing a lump in his throat he said, "It ought to be time to eat."

> *"God help Kaiser Bill!*
> *O-o-o old Uncle Sam.*
> *He's got the cavalry,*
> *He's got the infantry,*
> *He's got the artillery;*
> *And then by God we'll all go to Germany!*
> *God help Kaiser Bill!"*

The iron covers are clamped on the smoking-room windows, for no lights must show. So the air is dense with tobacco smoke and the reek of beer and champagne. In one corner they are playing poker with their coats off. All the chairs are full of sprawling young men who stamp their feet to the time, and bang their fists down so that the bottles dance on the tables.

"God help Kaiser Bill."

Sky and sea are opal grey. Martin is stretched on the deck in the bow of the boat with an unopened book beside him. He has never been so happy in his life. The future is nothing to him, the past is nothing to him. All his life is effaced in the grey languor of the sea, in the soft surge of the water about the ship's bow as she ploughs through the long swell, eastward. The tepid moisture of the Gulf Stream makes his clothes feel damp and his hair stick together into curls that straggle over his forehead. There are porpoises about, lazily tumbling in the swell, and flying-fish skim from one grey wave to another, and the bow rises and falls gently in rhythm with the surging sing-song of the broken water.

Martin has been asleep. As through infinite mists of greyness he looks back on the sharp hatreds and wringing desires of his life. Now a leaf seems to have been turned and a new white page spread before him, clean and unwritten on. At last things have come to pass.

And very faintly, like music heard across the water in the evening, blurred into strange harmonies, his old watchwords echo a little in his mind. Like the red flame

of the sunset setting fire to opal sea and sky, the old exal-
tation, the old flame that would consume to ashes all the
lies in the world, the trumpet-blast under which the
walls of Jericho would fall down, stirs and broods in the
womb of his grey lassitude. The bow rises and falls
gently in rhythm with the surging sing-song of the
broken water, as the steamer ploughs through the long
swell of the Gulf Stream, eastward.

"See that guy, the feller with the straw hat; he lost
five hundred dollars at craps last night."

"Some stakes."

It is almost dark. Sea and sky are glowing claret
colour, darkened to a cold bluish-green to westward. In a
corner of the deck a number of men are crowded in a
circle, while one shakes the dice in his hand with a
strange nervous quiver that ends in a snap of the fingers
as the white dice roll on the deck.

"Seven up."

From the smoking-room comes a sound of singing
and glasses banged on tables.

"Oh, we're bound for the Hamburg show,
To see the elephant and the wild kangaroo,
An' we'll all stick together
In fair or foul weather,
For we're going to see the damn show through!"

On the settee a sallow young man is shaking the ice in
a whisky-and-soda into a nervous tinkle as he talks:

"There's nothing they can do against this new gas.
. . . It just corrodes the lungs as if they were rotten
in a dead body. In the hospitals they just stand the poor
devils up against a wall and let them die. They say their
skin turns green and that it takes from five to seven days
to die—five to seven days of slow choking."

"Oh, but I think it's so splendid of you"—she bared
all her teeth, white and regular as those in a dentist's
show-case, in a smile as she spoke—"to come over this
way to help France."

"Perhaps it's only curiosity," muttered Martin.

"Oh no. . . . You're too modest. . . . What I mean
is that it's so splendid to have understood the issues.
. . . That's how I feel. I just told dad I'd have to come
and do my bit, as the English say."

"What are you going to do?"

"Something in Paris. I don't know just what, but I'll
certainly make myself useful somehow." She beamed at
him provocatively. "Oh, if only I was a man, I'd have
shouldered my gun the first day; indeed I would."

"But the issues were hardly . . . defined then," ven-
tured Martin.

"They didn't need to be. I hate those brutes. I've always hated the Germans, their language, their country,
everything about them. And now that they've done such
frightful things . . ."

"I wonder if it's all true . . ."

"True! Oh, of course it's all true; and lots more that it

hasn't been possible to print, that people have been ashamed to tell."

"They've gone pretty far," said Martin, laughing.

"If there are any left alive after the war they ought to be chloroformed. . . . And really I don't think it's patriotic or humane to take the atrocities so lightly. . . . But really, you must excuse me if you think me rude; I do get so excited and wrought up when I think of those frightful things. . . . I get quite beside myself; I'm sure you do too, in your heart. . . . Any red-blooded person would."

"Only I doubt . . ."

"But you're just playing into their hands if you do that. . . . Oh, dear, I'm quite beside myself, just thinking of it." She raised a small gloved hand to her pink cheek in a gesture of horror, and settled herself comfortably in her deck chair. "Really, I oughtn't to talk about it. I lose all self-control when I do. I hate them so it makes me quite ill. . . . The curs! The Huns! Let me tell you just one story. . . . I know it'll make your blood boil. It's absolutely authentic, too. I heard it before I left New York from a girl who's really the best friend I have on earth. She got it from a friend of hers who had got it directly from a little Belgian girl, poor little thing, who was in the convent at the time. . . . Oh, I don't see why they ever take any prisoners; I'd kill them all like mad dogs."

"What's the story?"

"Oh, I can't tell it. It upsets me too much. . . . No, that's silly, I've got to begin facing realities. . . . It was just when the Germans were taking Bruges, the Uhlans broke into this convent. . . . But I think it was in Louvain, not Bruges. . . . I have a wretched memory for names. . . . Well, they broke in, and took all those poor defenceless little girls . . ."

"There's the dinner-bell."

"Oh, so it is. I must run and dress. I'll have to tell you later. . . ."

Through half-closed eyes, Martin watched the fluttering dress and the backs of the neat little white shoes go jauntily down the deck.

The smoking-room again. Clink of glasses and chatter of confident voices. Two men talking over their glasses.

"They tell me that Paris is some city."

"The most immoral place in the world, before the war. Why, there are houses there where . . ." his voice sank into a whisper. The other man burst into loud guffaws.

"But the war's put an end to all that. They tell me that French people are regenerated, positively regenerated."

"They say the lack of food's something awful, that you can't get a square meal. They even eat horse."

"Did you hear what those fellows were saying about that new gas? Sounds frightful, don't it? I don't care a

thing about bullets, but that kind o' gives me cold feet.
. . . I don't give a damn about bullets, but that
gas . . ."

"That's why so many shoot their friends when
they're gassed. . . ."

"Say, you two, how about a hand of poker?"

A champagne cork pops.

"Jiminy, don't spill it all over me."

"Where we goin', boys?"

"Oh, we're going to the Hamburg show
To see the elephant and the wild kangaroo,
And we'll all stick together
In fair or foul weather,
For we're going to see the damn show through!"

Chapter II

BEFORE going to bed Martin had seen the lighthouses winking at the mouth of the Gironde, and had filled his lungs with the new, indefinably scented wind coming off the land. The sound of screaming whistles of tug-boats awoke him. Feet were tramping on the deck above his head. The shrill whine of a crane sounded in his ears and the throaty cry of men lifting something in unison.

Through his port-hole in the yet colourless dawn he saw the reddish water of a river with black-hulled sailing-boats on it and a few lanky little steamers of a pattern he had never seen before. Again he breathed deep of the new indefinable smell off the land.

Once on deck in the cold air, he saw through the faint light a row of houses beyond the low wharf buildings, grey mellow houses of four storeys with tiled roofs and intricate ironwork balconies, with balconies in which the ironwork had been carefully twisted by artisans long ago dead into gracefully modulated curves and spirals.

Some in uniform, some not, the ambulance men

marched to the station, through the grey streets of Bordeaux. Once a woman opened a window and crying, "Vive l'Amérique," threw out a bunch of roses and daisies. As they were rounding a corner, a man with a frockcoat on ran up and put his own hat on the head of one of the Americans who had none. In front of the station, waiting for the train, they sat at the little tables of cafés, lolling comfortably in the early morning sunlight, and drank beer and cognac.

Small railway carriages into which they were crowded so that their knees were pressed tight together —and outside, slipping by, blue-green fields, and poplars stalking out of the morning mist, and long drifts of poppies. Scarlet poppies, and cornflowers, and white daisies, and the red-tiled roofs and white walls of cottages, all against a background of glaucous green fields and hedges. Tours, Poitiers, Orléans. In the names of the stations rose old wars, until the floods of scarlet poppies seemed the blood of fighting men slaughtered through all time. At last, in the gloaming, Paris, and, in crossing a bridge over the Seine, a glimpse of the two linked towers of Notre Dame, rosy grey in the grey mist up the river.

"Say, these women here get my goat."
"How do you mean?"
"Well, I was at the Olympia with Johnson and that

crowd. They just pester the life out of you there. I'd heard that Paris was immoral, but nothing like this."

"It's the war."

"But the Jane I went with . . ."

"Why didn't you spend the night with her?"

"I got sort o' disgusted, and then I began to sober up."

"You'd better take precautions."

"You bet. . . . It's sort o' disgusting, though, isn't it?"

"Looks like every woman you saw walking on the street was a whore. They certainly are good-lookers though."

"King and his gang are all being sent back to the States."

"I'll be darned! They sure have been drunk ever since they got off the steamer."

"Raised hell in Maxim's last night. They tried to clean up the place and the police came. They were all soused to the gills and tried to make everybody there sing the 'Star Spangled Banner.' "

"Damn fool business."

Martin Howe sat at a table on the sidewalk under the brown awning of a restaurant. Opposite in the last topaz-clear rays of the sun, the foliage of the Jardin du Luxembourg shone bright green above deep alleys of bluish shadow. From the pavements in front of the mauve-coloured houses rose little kiosks with advertisements in bright orange and vermilion and blue. In the middle of the triangle formed by the streets and the garden was a round pool of jade water. Martin leaned back in his chair looking dreamily out through half-closed eyes, breathing deep now and then of the musty scent of Paris, that mingled with the melting freshness of the wild strawberries on the plate before him.

As he stared in front of him two figures crossed his field of vision. A woman swathed in black crepe veils was helping a soldier to a seat at the next table. He found himself staring in a face, a face that still had some of the chubbiness of boyhood. Between the pale-brown frightened eyes, where the nose should have been, was a triangular black patch that ended in some mechanical contrivance with shiny little black metal rods that took the place of the jaw. He could not take his eyes from the soldier's eyes, that were like those of a hurt animal, full of meek dismay. Someone plucked at Martin's arm, and he turned suddenly, fearfully.

A bent old woman was offering him flowers with a jerky curtsey.

"Just a rose, for good luck?"

"No, thank you."

"It will bring you happiness."

He took a couple of the reddest of the roses.

"Do you understand the language of flowers?"

"No."

"I shall teach you. . . . Thank you so much. . . . Thank you so much."

She added a few large daisies to the red roses in his hand.

"These will bring you love. . . . But another time I shall teach you the language of flowers, the language of love."

She curtseyed again, and began making her way jerkily down the sidewalk, jingling his silver in her hand.

He stuck the roses and daisies in the belt of his uniform and sat with the green flame of Chartreuse in a little glass before him, staring into the gardens, where the foliage was becoming blue and lavender with evening, and the shadows darkened to grey-purple and black. Now and then he glanced furtively, with shame, at the man at the next table. When the restaurant closed he wandered through the unlighted streets towards the river, listening to the laughs and conversations that bubbled like the sparkle in Burgundy through the purple summer night.

But wherever he looked in the comradely faces of young men, in the beckoning eyes of women, he saw the brown hurt eyes of the soldier, and the triangular black patch where the nose should have been.

Chapter III

At Epernay the station was wrecked; the corrugated tin of the roof hung in strips over the crumbled brick walls.

"They say the Boches came over last night. They killed a lot of permissionaires."

"That river's the Marne."

"Gosh, is it? Let me get to the winder."

The third-class car, joggling along on a flat wheel, was full of the smell of sweat and sour wine. Outside, yellow-green and blue-green, crossed by long processions of poplars, aflame with vermilion and carmine of poppies, the countryside slipped by. At a station where the train stopped on a siding, they could hear a faint hollow sound in the distance: guns.

Croix de Guerre had been given out that day at the automobile park at Châlons. There was an unusually big dinner at the wooden tables in the narrow portable barracks, and during the last course the General passed through and drank a glass of champagne to the health of all present. Everybody had on his best uniform and sweated hugely in the narrow, airless building, from the wine and the champagne and the thick stew, thickly seasoned, that made the dinner's main course.

"We are all one large family," said the General from the end of the barracks . . . "to France."

That night the wail of a siren woke Martin suddenly and made him sit up in his bunk trembling, wondering where he was. Like the shriek of a woman in a nightmare, the wail of the siren rose and rose and then dropped in pitch and faded throbbingly out.

"Don't flash a light there. It's Boche planes."

Outside the night was cold, with a little light from a waned moon.

"See the shrapnel!" someone cried.

"The Boche has a Mercedes motor," said someone else. "You can tell by the sound of it."

"They say one of their planes chased an ambulance ten miles along a straight road the other day, trying to get it with a machinegun. The man who was driving got away, but he had shell-shock afterwards."

"Did he really?"

"Oh, I'm goin' to turn in. God, these French nights are cold!"

The rain pattered hard with unfaltering determination on the roof of the little arbour. Martin lolled over the rough board table, resting his chin on his clasped

hands, looking through the tinkling bead curtains of the
rain towards the other end of the weed-grown garden,
where, under a canvas shelter, the cooks were moving
about in front of two black steaming cauldrons.
Through the fresh scent of rain-beaten leaves came a
greasy smell of soup. He was thinking of the jolly
wedding-parties that must have drunk and danced in
this garden before the war, of the lovers who must have
sat in that very arbour, pressing sunburned cheek
against sunburned cheek, twining hands callous with
work in the fields. A man broke suddenly into the
arbour behind Martin and stood flicking the water off
his uniform with his cap. His sand-coloured hair was
wet and was plastered in little spikes to his broad forehead, a forehead that was the entablature of a determined rock-hewn face.

"Hello," said Martin, twisting his head to look at the
newcomer. "You section twenty-four?"

"Yes. . . . Ever read 'Alice in Wonderland'?" asked
the wet man, sitting down abruptly at the table.

"Yes, indeed."

"Doesn't this remind you of it?"

"What?"

"This war business. Why, I keep thinking I'm going
to meet the rabbit who put butter in his watch round
every corner."

"It was the best butter."

"That's the hell of it."

"When's your section leaving here?" asked Martin, picking up the conversation after a pause during which they'd both stared out into the rain. They could hear almost constantly the grinding roar of camions on the road behind the café and the slither of their wheels through the mud-puddles where the road turned into the village.

"How the devil should I know?"

"Somebody had dope this morning that we'd leave here for Soissons to-morrow." Martin's words tailed off into a convictionless mumble.

"It surely is different than you'd pictured it, isn't it, now?"

They sat looking at each other while the big drops from the leaky roof smacked on the table or splashed cold in their faces.

"What do you think of all this, anyway?" said the wet man suddenly, lowering his voice stealthily.

"I don't know. I never did expect it to be what we were taught to believe. . . . Things aren't."

"But you can't have guessed that it was like this . . . like Alice in Wonderland, like an ill-intentioned Drury Lane pantomime, like all the dusty futility of Barnum and Bailey's Circus."

"No, I thought it would be hair-raising," said Martin.

"Think, man, think of all the oceans of lies through all the ages that must have been necessary to make this possible! Think of this new particular vintage of lies that has been so industriously pumped out of the press and the pulpit. Doesn't it stagger you?"

Martin nodded.

"Why, lies are like a sticky juice overspreading the world, a living, growing flypaper to catch and gum the wings of every human soul. . . . And the little helpless buzzings of honest, liberal, kindly people, aren't they like the thin little noise flies make when they're caught?"

"I agree with you that the little thin noise is very silly," said Martin.

Martin slammed down the hood of the car and stood upright. A cold stream of rain ran down the sleeves of his slicker and dripped from his greasy hands.

Infantry tramped by, the rain spattering with a cold glitter on grey helmets, on gun-barrels, on the straps of equipment. Red sweating faces, drooping under the hard rims of helmets, turned to the ground with the struggle with the weight of equipment; rows and patches of faces were the only warmth in the desolation of putty-coloured mud and bowed mud-coloured bodies and dripping mud-coloured sky. In the cold colourlessness they were delicate and feeble as the faces of children, rosy and soft under the splattering of mud and the shagginess of unshaven beards.

Martin rubbed the back of his hand against his face. His skin was like that, too, soft as the petals of flowers, soft and warm amid all this dead mud, amid all this hard mud-covered steel.

He leant against the side of the car, his ears full of the heavy shuffle, of the jingle of equipment, of the splashing in puddles of water-soaked boots, and watched the endless rosy patches of faces moving by, the faces that drooped towards the dripping boots that rose and fell, churning into froth the soupy, putty-coloured mud of the road.

The schoolmaster's garden was full of late roses and marigolds, all parched and bleached by the thick layer of dust that was over them. Next to the vine-covered trellis that cut the garden off from the road stood a green table and a few cane chairs. The schoolmaster, something charmingly eighteenth-century about the cut of his breeches and the calves of his legs in their thick woollen golf-stockings, led the way, a brown pitcher of wine in his hand. Martin Howe and the black-haired, brown-faced boy from New Orleans who was his carmate followed him. Then came a little grey woman in a pink knitted shawl, carrying a tray with glasses.

"In the Verdunois our wine is not very good," said the schoolmaster, bowing them into chairs. "It is thin and cold like the climate. To your health, gentlemen."

"To France."

"To America."

"And down with the Boches."

In the pale yellow light that came from among the dark clouds that passed over the sky, the wine had the chilly gleam of yellow diamonds.

"Ah, you should have seen that road in 1916," said the schoolmaster, drawing a hand over his watery blue eyes. "That, you know, is the Voie Sacrée, the sacred way that saved Verdun. All day, all day, a double line of camions went up, full of ammunition and ravitaillement and men."

"Oh, the poor boys, we saw so many go up," came the voice, dry as the rustling of the wind in the vine-leaves, of the grey old woman who stood leaning against the schoolmaster's chair, looking out through a gap in the trellis at the rutted road so thick with dust, "and never have we seen one of them come back."

"It was for France."

"But this was a nice village before the war. From Verdun to Bar-le-Duc, the Courrier des Postes used to tell us, there was no such village, so clean and with such fine orchards." The old woman leaned over the school-master's shoulder, joining eagerly in the conversation.

"Even now the fruit is very fine," said Martin.

"But you soldiers, you steal it all," said the old woman, throwing out her arms. "You leave us nothing, nothing."

"We don't begrudge it," said the schoolmaster, "all we have is our country's."

"We shall starve then. . . ."

As she spoke the glasses on the table shook. With a roar of heavy wheels and a grind of gears a camion went by.

"O good God!" The old woman looked out on to the road with terror in her face, blinking her eyes in the thick dust.

Roaring with heavy wheels, grinding with gears, throbbing with motors, camion after camion went by, slowly, stridently. The men packed into the camions had broken through the canvas covers and leaned out waving their arms and shouting.

"Oh, the poor children," said the old woman, wringing her hands, her voice lost in the roar and the shouting.

"They should not destroy property that way," said the schoolmaster. . . . "Last year it was dreadful. There were mutinies."

Martin sat, his chair tilted back, his hands trembling, staring with compressed lips at the men who jolted by on the strident, throbbing camions. A word formed in his mind: tumbrils.

In some trucks the men were drunk and singing, waving their bidons in the air, shouting at people along the road, crying out all sorts of things: "Get to the front!" "Into the trenches with them!" "Down with the war!" In others they sat quiet, faces corpse-like with dust. Through the gap in the trellis Martin stared at them, noting intelligent faces, beautiful faces, faces brutally gay, miserable faces like those of sobbing drunkards.

At last the convoy passed and the dust settled again on the rutted road.

"Oh, the poor children!" said the old woman. "They know they are going to death."

They tried to hide their agitation. The schoolmaster poured out more wine.

"Yes," said Martin, "there are fine orchards on the hills round here."

"You should be here when the plums are ripe," said the schoolmaster.

A tall bearded man, covered with dust to the eyelashes, in the uniform of a commandant, stepped into the garden.

"My dear friends!" He shook hands with the schoolmaster and the old woman and saluted the two Americans. "I could not pass without stopping a moment. We are going up to an attack. We have the honour to take the lead."

"You will have a glass of wine, won't you?"

"With great pleasure."

"Julie, fetch a bottle, you know which. . . . How is the morale?"

"Perfect."

"I thought they looked a little discontented."

"No. . . . It's always like that. . . . They were yelling at some gendarmes. If they strung up a couple it would serve them right, dirty beasts."

"You soldiers are all one against the gendarmes."

"Yes. We fight the enemy but we hate the gendarmes." The commandant rubbed his hands, drank his wine and laughed.

"Hah! There's the next convoy. I must go."

"Good luck."

The commandant shrugged his shoulders, clicked his heels together at the garden gate, saluted, smiling, and was gone.

Again the village street was full of the grinding roar and throb of camions, full of a frenzy of wheels and drunken shouting.

"Give us a drink, you."

"We're the train de luxe, we are."

"Down with the war!"

And the old grey woman wrung her hands and said:

"Oh, the poor children, they know they are going to death!"

Chapter IV

M ARTIN, rolled up in his bedroll on the floor of the empty hayloft, woke with a start.

"Say, Howe!" Tom Randolph, who lay next him, was pressing his hand. "I think I heard a shell go over."

As he spoke there came a shrill, loudening whine, and an explosion that shook the barn. A little dirt fell down on Martin's face.

"Say, fellers, that was damn near," came a voice from the floor of the barn.

"We'd better go over to the quarry."

"Oh, hell, I was sound asleep!"

A vicious shriek overhead and a shaking snort of explosion.

"Gee, that was in the house behind us. . . ."

"I smell gas."

"Ye damn fool, it's carbide."

"One of the Frenchmen said it was gas."

"All right, fellers, put on your masks."

Outside there was a sickly rough smell in the air that mingled strangely with the perfume of the cool night, musical with the gurgling of the stream through the little valley where their barn was. They crouched in a quarry by the roadside, a straggling, half-naked group, and watched the flashes in the sky northward, where artillery along the lines kept up a continuous hammering drum-beat. Over their head shells shrieked at two-minute intervals, to explode with a rattling ripping sound in the village on the other side of the valley.

"Damn foolishness," muttered Tom Randolph in his rich Southern voice. "Why don't those damn gunners go to sleep and let us go to sleep? . . . They must be tired like we are."

A shell burst in a house on the crest of the hill opposite, so that they saw the flash against the starry night sky. In the silence that followed, the moaning shriek of a man came faintly across the valley.

Martin sat on the steps of the dugout, looking up the shattered shaft of a tree, from the top of which a few ribbons of bark fluttered against the mauve evening sky. In the quiet he could hear the voices of men chatting in the dark below him, and a sound of someone whistling as he worked. Now and then, like some ungainly bird, a high calibre shell trundled through the air overhead; after its noise had completely died away would come the thud of the explosion. It was like battledore and shuttlecock, these huge masses whirling through the evening far above his head, now from one side, now from the other. It gave him somehow a cosy feeling of safety, as if he were under some sort of a bridge over which freight-cars were shunted madly to and fro.

The doctor in charge of the post came up and sat beside Martin. He was a small brown man with slim black moustaches that curved like the horns of a long-horn steer. He stood on tip-toe on the top step and peered about in every direction with an air of ownership, then sat down again and began talking briskly.

"We are exactly four hundred and five mètres from the Boche. . . . Five hundred mètres from here they are drinking beer and saying, 'Hoch der Kaiser.'"

"About as much as we're saying 'Vive la République,' I should say."

"Who knows? But it is quiet here, isn't it? It's quieter here than in Paris."

"The sky is very beautiful to-night."

"They say they're shelling the Etat-Major to-day. Damned embusqués; it'll do them good to get a bit of their own medicine."

Martin did not answer. He was crossing in his mind the four hundred and five mètres to the first Boche listening-post. Next beyond the abris was the latrine from which a puff of wind brought now and then a nauseous stench. Then there was the tin roof, crumpled as if by a hand, that had been a cook shack. That was just behind the second line trenches that zig-zagged in and out of great abscesses of wet, upturned clay along the crest of a little hill. The other day he had been there, and had clambered up the oily clay where the boyau had caved in, and from the level of the ground had looked for an anxious minute or two at the tangle of trenches and pitted gangrened soil in the direction of the German outposts. And all along these random gashes in the mucky clay were men, feet and legs huge from clotting after clotting of clay, men with greyish-green faces scarred by lines of strain and fear and boredom as the hillside was scarred out of all semblance by the trenches and the shell-holes.

"We are well off here," said the doctor again. "I have not had a serious case all day."

"Up in the front line there's a place where they've planted rhubarb. . . . You know, where the hillside is beginning to get rocky."

"It was the Boche who did that. . . . We took that slope from them two months ago. . . . How does it grow?"

"They say the gas makes the leaves shrivel," said Martin, laughing.

He looked long at the little ranks of clouds that had begun to fill the sky, like ruffles on a woman's dress. Might not it really be, he kept asking himself, that the sky was a beneficent goddess who would stoop gently out of the infinite spaces and lift him to her breast, where he could lie amid the amber-fringed ruffles of cloud and look curiously down at the spinning ball of the earth? It might have beauty if he were far enough away to clear his nostrils of the stench of pain.

"It is funny," said the little doctor suddenly, "to think how much nearer we are, in state of mind, in everything, to the Germans than to anyone else."

"You mean that the soldiers in the trenches are all further from the people at home than from each other, no matter what side they are on."

The little doctor nodded.

"God, it's so stupid! Why can't we go over and talk to them? Nobody's fighting about anything. . . . God, it's so hideously stupid!" cried Martin, suddenly carried away, helpless in the flood of his passionate revolt.

"Life is stupid," said the little doctor sententiously.

Suddenly from the lines came a splutter of machine-guns.

"Evensong!" cried the little doctor. "Ah, but here's business. You'd better get your car ready, my friend."

The brancardiers set the stretcher down at the top of the steps that led to the door of the dugout, so that Martin found himself looking into the lean, sensitive face, stained a little with blood about the mouth, of the wounded man. His eyes followed along the shapeless bundles of blood-flecked uniform till they suddenly turned away. Where the middle of the man had been, where had been the curved belly and the genitals, where the thighs had joined with a strong swerving of muscles to the trunk, was a depression, a hollow pool of blood, that glinted a little in the cold diffusion of grey light from the west.

The rain beat hard on the window-panes of the little room and hissed down the chimney into the smouldering fire that sent up thick green smoke. At a plain oak table before the fireplace sat Martin Howe and Tom Randolph, Tom Randolph with his sunburned hands with their dirty nails spread flat and his head resting on the table between them, so that Martin could see the stiff black hair on top of his head and the dark nape of his neck going into shadow under the collar of the flannel shirt.

"Oh, God, it's too damned absurd! An arrangement for mutual suicide and no damned other thing," said Randolph, raising his head.

"A certain jolly asinine grotesqueness, though. I mean, if you were God and could look at it like that . . . Oh, Randy, why do they enjoy hatred so?"

"A question of taste . . . as the lady said when she kissed the cow."

"But it isn't. It isn't natural for people to hate that way, it can't be. It even disgusts the perfectly stupid damn-fool people, like Higgins, who believes that the Bible was written in God's own handwriting and that the newspapers tell the truth."

"It makes me sick at ma stomach, Howe, to talk to one of those Hun-hatin' women, if they're male or female."

"It is a stupid affair, *la vie*, as the doctor at P.i. said yesterday. . . ."

"Hell, yes. . . ."

They sat silent, watching the rain beat on the window, and run down in sparkling finger-like streams.

"What I can't get over is these Frenchwomen." Randolph threw back his head and laughed. "They're so bloody frank. Did I tell you about what happened to me at that last village on the Verdun road?"

"No."

"I was lyin' down for a nap under a plumtree, a wonderfully nice place near a li'l brook an' all, an' suddenly that crazy Jane. . . . You know the one that used to throw stones at us out of that broken-down house at the corner of the road. . . . Anyway, she lays down beside me an' before I am properly awake is all cuddled up an' ready for business. I had a regular wrastlin' match gettin' away from her."

"Funny position for you to be in, getting away from a woman."

"But doesn't that strike you funny? Why, down where I come from a drunken mulatto woman wouldn't act like that. They all keep up a fake of not wantin' your attentions." His black eyes sparkled, and he laughed his deep ringing laugh, that made the withered woman smile as she set an omelette before them.

"Voilà, messieurs," she said with a grand air, as if it were a boar's head that she was serving.

Three French infantrymen came into the café, shaking the rain off their shoulders.

"Nothing to drink but champagne at four francs fifty," shouted Howe. "Dirty night out, isn't it?"

"We'll drink that, then!"

Howe and Randolph moved up and they all sat at the same table.

"Fortune of war?"

"Oh, the war, what do you think of the war?" cried Martin.

"What do you think of the peste? You think about saving your skin."

"What's amusing about us is that we three have all saved our skins together," said one of the Frenchmen.

"Yes. We are of the same class," said another, holding up his thumb. "Mobilised same day." He held up his first finger. "Same company." He held up a second finger. Wounded by the same shell. . . . Evacuated to the same hospital. Convalescence at same time. . . . Réformé to the same depôt behind the lines."

"Didn't all marry the same girl, did you, to make it complete?" asked Randolph.

They all shouted with laughter until the glasses along the bar rang.

"Not exactly, but we were once in a town where there was only one woman. Which amounted to the same. . . ."

"You must be Athos, Porthos, and d'Artagnan."

"Some more champagne, madame, for the three musketeers," sang Randolph in a sort of operatic yodle.

"All I have left is this," said the withered woman, setting a bottle down on the table.

"Is that poison?"

"It's cognac, it's very good cognac," said the old woman seriously.

"C'est du cognac! Vive le roi cognac!" everybody shouted.

> "Au plein de mon cognac
> Qu'il fait bon, fait bon, fait bon,
> Au plein de mon cognac
> Qu'il fait bon dormir."

"Down with the war! Who can sing the 'Internationale'?"

"Not so much noise, I beg you, gentlemen," came the withered woman's whining voice. "It's after hours. Last week I was fined. Next time I'll be closed up."

The night was black when Martin and Randolph, after lengthy and elaborate farewells, started down the muddy road towards the hospital. They staggered along the slippery footpath beside the road, splashed every instant with mud by camions, huge and dark, that roared grindingly by. They ran and skipped arm-in-arm and shouted at the top of their lungs:

> "*Auprès de ma blonde,*
> *Qu'il fait bon, fait bon, fait bon,*
> *Auprès de ma blonde,*
> *Qu'il fait bon dormir.*"

A stench of sweat and filth and formaldehyde caught them by the throat as they went into the hospital tent, gave them a sense of feverish bodies of men stretched all about them, stirring in pain.

"A car for la Bassée, Ambulance 4," said the orderly.

Howe got himself up off the hospital stretcher, shoving his flannel shirt back into his breeches, put on his coat and belt and felt his way to the door, stumbling over the legs of sleeping brancardiers as he went. Men swore in their sleep and turned over heavily. At the door he waited a minute, then shouted:

"Coming, Tom?"

"Too damn sleepy," came Randolph's voice from under a blanket.

"I've got cigarettes, Tom. I'll smoke 'em all up if you don't come."

"All right, I'll come."

"Less noise, name of God!" cried a man, sitting up on his stretcher.

After the hospital, smelling of chloride and blankets and reeking clothes, the night air was unbelievably sweet. Like a gilt fringe on a dark shawl, a little band of brightness had appeared in the east.

"Some dawn, Howe, ain't it?"

As they were going off, their motor chugging regularly, an orderly said:

"It's a special case. Go for orders to the commandant."

Colours formed gradually out of chaotic grey as the day brightened. At the dressing-station an attendant ran up to the car.

"Oh, you're for the special case? Have you anything to tie a man with?"

"No, why?"

"It's nothing. He just tried to stab the sergeant-major."

The attendant raised a fist and tapped on his head as if knocking on a door. "It's nothing. He's quieter now."

"What caused it?"

"Who knows? There is so much. . . . He says he must kill everyone. . . ."

"Are you ready?"

A lieutenant of the medical corps came to the door and looked out. He smiled reassuringly at Martin Howe. "He's not violent any more. And we'll send two guardians."

77

A sergeant came out with a little packet which he handed to Martin.

"That's his. Will you give it to them at the hospital at Fourreaux? And here's his knife. They can give it back to him when he gets better. He has an idea he ought to kill everyone he sees. . . . Funny idea."

The sun had risen and shone gold across the broad rolling lands, so that the hedges and the poplar-rows cast long blue shadows over the fields. The man, with a guardian on either side of him who cast nervous glances to the right and to the left, came placidly, eyes straight in front of him, out of the dark interior of the dressing-station. He was a small man with moustaches and small, goodnatured lips puffed into an o-shape. At the car he turned and saluted.

"Good-bye, my lieutenant. Thank you for your kindness," he said.

"Good-bye, old chap," said the lieutenant.

The little man stood up in the car, looking about him anxiously.

"I've lost my knife. Where's my knife?"

The guards got in behind him with a nervous, sheepish air. They answered reassuringly, "The driver's got it. The American's got it."

"Good."

The orderly jumped on the seat with the two Americans to show the way. He whispered in Martin's ear:

"He's crazy. He says that to stop the war you must kill everybody, kill everybody."

In an open valley that sloped between hills covered with beech-woods, stood the tall abbey, a Gothic nave and apse with beautifully traced windows, with the ruin of a very ancient chapel on one side, and crossing the back, a well-proportioned Renaissance building that had been a dormitory. The first time that Martin saw the abbey, it towered in ghostly perfection above a low veil of mist that made the valley seem a lake in the shining moonlight. The lines were perfectly quiet, and when he stopped the motor of his ambulance, he could hear the wind rustling among the beech-woods. Except for the dirty smell of huddled soldiers that came now and then in drifts along with the cool woodscents, there might have been no war at all. In the soft moonlight the great traceried windows and the buttresses and the high-pitched roof seemed as gorgeously untroubled by decay as if the carvings on the cusps and arches had just come from under the careful chisels of the Gothic workmen.

"And you say we've progressed," he whispered to Tom Randolph.

"God, it is fine."

They wandered up and down the road a long time, silently, looking at the tall apse of the abbey, breathing the cool night air, moist with mist, in which now and then was the huddled, troubling smell of soldiers. At last the moon, huge and swollen with gold, set behind the wooded hills, and they went back to the car, where they rolled up in their blankets and went to sleep.

Behind the square lantern that rose over the crossing, there was a trap door in the broken tile roof, from which you could climb to the observation post in the lantern. Here, half on the roof and half on the platform behind the trap door, Martin would spend the long summer afternoons when there was no call for the ambulance, looking at the Gothic windows of the lantern and the blue sky beyond, where huge soft clouds passed slowly over, darkening the green of the woods and of the weed-grown fields of the valley with their moving shadows.

There was almost no activity on that part of the front. A couple of times a day a few snapping discharges would come from the seventy-fives of the battery behind the abbey, and the woods would resound like a shaken harp as the shells passed over to explode on the crest of the hill that blocked the end of the valley where the Boches were.

Martin would sit and dream of the quiet lives the monks must have passed in their beautiful abbey so far away in the Forest of the Argonne, digging and planting in the rich lands of the valley, making flowers bloom in the garden, of which traces remained in the huge beds of sunflowers and orange marigolds that bloomed along the walls of the dormitory. In a room in the top of the house he had found a few torn remnants of books; there must have been a library in the old days, rows and rows of musty-smelling volumes in rich brown calf worn by use to a velvet softness, and in cream-coloured parchment where the fingermarks of generations showed brown; huge psalters with notes and chants illuminated in green and ultramarine and gold; manuscripts out of the Middle Ages with strange script and pictures in pure vivid colours; lives of saints, thoughts polished by years of quiet meditation of old divines; old romances of chivalry; tales of blood and death and love where the crude agony of life was seen through a dawn-like mist of gentle beauty.

"God! if there were somewhere nowadays where you could flee from all this stupidity, from all this cant of governments, and this hideous reiteration of hatred, this strangling hatred . . ." he would say to himself, and see himself working in the fields, copying parchments in quaint letterings, drowsing his feverish desires to calm in the deep-throated passionate chanting of the endless offices of the Church.

One afternoon towards evening as he lay on the tiled roof with his shirt open so that the sun warmed his throat and chest, half asleep in the beauty of the building and of the woods and the clouds that drifted over-head, he heard a strain from the organ in the church: a few deep notes in broken rhythm that filled him with wonder, as if he had suddenly been transported back to the quiet days of the monks. The rhythm changed in an instant, and through the squeakiness of shattered pipes came a swirl of fake-oriental ragtime that resounded like mocking laughter in the old vaults and arches. He went down into the church and found Tom Randolph playing on the little organ, pumping desperately with his feet.

"Hello! Impiety I call it; putting your lustful tunes into that pious old organ."

"I bet the ole monks had a merry time, lecherous ole devils," said Tom, playing away.

"If there were monasteries nowadays," said Martin, "I think I'd go into one."

"But there are. I'll end up in one, most like, if they don't put me in jail first. I reckon every living soul would be a candidate for either one if it'd get them out of this God-damned war."

There was a shriek overhead that reverberated strangely in the vaults of the church and made the swallows nesting there fly in and out through the glassless windows. Tom Randolph stopped on a wild chord.

"Guess they don't like me playin'."

"That one didn't explode though."

"That one did, by gorry," said Randolph, getting up off the floor, where he had thrown himself automatically. A shower of tiles came rattling off the roof, and through the noise could be heard the frightened squeaking of the swallows.

"I am afraid that winged somebody."

"They must have got wind of the ammunition dump in the cellar."

"Hell of a place to put a dressing-station—over an ammunition dump!"

The whitewashed room used as a dressing-station had a smell of blood stronger than the chloride. A doctor was leaning over a stretcher on which Martin caught a glimpse of two naked legs with flecks of blood on the white skin, as he passed through on his way to the car.

"Three stretcher-cases for Les Islettes. Very softly," said the attendant, handing him the papers.

Jolting over the shell-pitted road, the car wound slowly through unploughed weed-grown fields. At every jolt came a rasping groan from the wounded men.

As they came back towards the front posts again, they found all the batteries along the road firing. The air was a chaos of explosions that jabbed viciously into their ears, above the reassuring purr of the motor. Nearly to the abbey a soldier stopped them.

"Put the car behind the trees and get into a dugout. They're shelling the abbey."

As he spoke a whining shriek grew suddenly loud over their heads. The soldier threw himself flat in the muddy road. The explosion brought gravel about their ears and made a curious smell of almonds.

Crowded in the door of the dugout in the hill opposite they watched the abbey as shell after shell tore through the roof or exploded in the strong buttresses of the apse. Dust rose high above the roof and filled the air with an odour of damp tiles and plaster. The woods resounded in a jangling tremor, with the batteries that started firing one after the other.

"God, I hate them for that!" said Randolph between his teeth.

"What do you want? It's an observation post."

"I know, but damn it!"

There was a series of explosions; a shell fragment whizzed past their heads.

"It's not safe there. You'd better come in all the way," someone shouted from within the dugout.

"I want to see; damn it. . . . I'm goin' to stay and see it out, Howe. That place meant a hell of a lot to me." Randolph blushed as he spoke.

Another bunch of shells crashing so near together they did not hear the scream. When the cloud of dust blew away, they saw that the lantern had fallen in on the roof of the apse, leaving only one wall and the tracery of a window, of which the shattered carving stood out cream-white against the reddish evening sky.

There was a lull in the firing. A few swallows still wheeled about the walls, giving shrill little cries.

They saw the flash of a shell against the sky as it exploded in the part of the tall roof that still remained. The roof crumpled and fell in, and again dust hid the abbey.

"Oh, I hate this!" said Tom Randolph. "But the question is, what's happened to our grub? The popote is buried four feet deep in Gothic art. . . . Damn fool idea, putting a dressing-station over an ammunition dump."

"Is the car hit?" The orderly came up to them.

"Don't think so."

"Good. Four stretcher-cases for 42 at once."

At night in a dugout. Five men playing cards about a lamp-flame that blows from one side to the other in the gusty wind that puffs every now and then down the mouth of the dugout and whirls round it like something alive trying to beat a way out.

Each time the lamp blows the shadows of the five heads writhe upon the corrugated tin ceiling. In the distance, like kettle-drums beaten for a dance, a constant reverberation of guns.

Martin Howe, stretched out in the straw of one of the bunks, watches their faces in the flickering shadows. He wishes he had the patience to play too. No, perhaps it is better to look on; it would be so silly to be killed in the middle of one of those grand gestures one makes in slamming the card down that takes the trick. Suddenly he thinks of all the lives that must, in these last three years, have ended in that grand gesture. It is too silly. He seems to see their poor lacerated souls, clutching their greasy dogeared cards, climb to a squalid Valhalla, and there, in tobacco-stinking, sweat-stinking rooms, like those of the little cafés behind the lines, sit in groups of five, shuffling, dealing, taking tricks, always with the same slam of the cards on the table, pausing now and then to scratch their louse-eaten flesh.

At this moment, how many men, in all the long Golgotha that stretches from Belfort to the sea, must be trying to cheat their boredom and their misery with that grand gesture of slamming the cards down to take a trick, while in their ears, like tom-toms, pounds the death-dance of the guns.

Martin lies on his back looking up at the curved corrugated ceiling of the dugout, where the shadows of the five heads writhe in fantastic shapes. Is it death they are playing, that they are so merry when they take a trick?

Chapter V

THE three planes gleamed like mica in the intense blue of the sky. Round about the shrapnel burst in little puffs like cotton-wool. A shout went up from the soldiers who stood in groups in the street of the ruined town. A whistle split the air, followed by a rending snort that tailed off into the moaning of a wounded man.

"By damn, they're nervy. They dropped a bomb."

"I should say they did."

"The dirty bastards, to get a fellow who's going on permission. Now if they beaded you on the way back you wouldn't care."

In the sky an escadrille of French planes had appeared and the three German specks had vanished, followed by a trail of little puffs of shrapnel. The indigo dome of the afternoon sky was full of a distant snoring of motors.

The train screamed outside the station and the permissionaires ran for the platform, their packed musettes bouncing at their hips.

The dark boulevards, with here and there a blue lamp lighting up a bench and a few tree-trunks, or a faint glow from inside a closed café where a boy in shirt-sleeves is sweeping the floor. Crowds of soldiers, Belgians, Americans, Canadians, civilians with canes and straw hats and well-dressed women on their arms, shop-girls in twos and threes laughing with shrill, merry voices; and everywhere girls of the street, giggling alluringly in hoarse, dissipated tones, clutching the arms of drunken soldiers, tilting themselves temptingly in men's way as they walk along. Cigarettes and cigars make spots of reddish light, and now and then a match lighted makes a man's face stand out in yellow relief and glints red in the eyes of people round about.

Drunk with their freedom, with the jangle of voices, with the rustle of trees in the faint light, with the scents of women's hair and cheap perfumes, Howe and Randolph stroll along slowly, down one side to the shadowy columns of the Madeleine, where a few flower-women still offer roses, scenting the darkness, then back again past the Opéra towards the Porte St. Martin, lingering to look in the offered faces of women, to listen to snatches of talk, to chatter laughingly with girls who squeeze their arms with impatience.

"I'm goin' to find the prettiest girl in Paris, and then you'll see the dust fly, Howe, old man."

The hors d'œuvres came on a circular three-tiered stand; red strips of herrings and silver anchovies, salads where green peas and bits of carrot lurked under golden layers of sauce, sliced tomatoes, potato salad green-specked with parsley, hard-boiled eggs barely visible under thickness of vermilion-tinged dressing, olives, radishes, discs of sausage of many different forms and colours, complicated bundles of spiced salt fish, and, forming the apex, a fat terra-cotta jar of pâté de foie gras. Howe poured out pale-coloured Chablis.

"I used to think that down home was the only place they knew how to live, but oh, boy . . ." said Tom Randolph, breaking a little loaf of bread that made a merry crackling sound.

"It's worth starving to death on singe and pinard for four months."

After the hors d'œuvres had been taken away, leaving them Rabelaisianly gay, with a joyous sense of orgy, came sole hidden in a cream-coloured sauce with mussels in it.

"After the war, Howe, ole man, let's riot all over Europe; I'm getting a taste for this sort of livin'."

"You can play the fiddle, can't you, Tom?"

"Enough to scrape out *Auprès de ma blonde* on a bet."

"Then we'll wander about and you can support me. . . . Or else I'll dress as a monkey and you can fiddle and I'll gather the pennies."

"By gum, that'd be great sport."

"Look, we must have some red wine with the veal."

"Let's have Mâcon."

"All the same to me as long as there's plenty of it."

Their round table with its white cloth and its bottles of wine and its piles of ravished artichoke leaves was the centre of a noisy, fantastic world. Ever since the orgy of the hors d'œuvres things had been evolving to grotesqueness, faces, whites of eyes, twisted red of lips, crow-like forms of waiters, colours of hats and uniforms, all involved and jumbled in the melée of talk and clink and clatter.

The red hand of the waiter pouring the Chartreuse, green like a stormy sunset, into small glasses before them broke into the vivid imaginings that had been unfolding in their talk through dinner. No, they had been saying, it could not go on; some day amid the rending crash of shells and the whine of shrapnel fragments, people everywhere, in all uniforms, in trenches, packed in camions, in stretchers, in hospitals, crowded behind guns, involved in telephone apparatus, generals at their dinner-tables, colonels sipping liqueurs, majors developing photographs, would jump to their feet and burst out laughing at the solemn inanity, at the stupid, vicious pomposity of what they were doing. Laughter would untune the sky. It would be a new progress of Bacchus. Drunk with laughter at the sudden vision of the silliness of the world, officers and soldiers, prisoners working on the roads, deserters being driven towards the trenches would throw down their guns and their spades and their heavy packs, and start marching, or driving in artillery waggons or in camions, staff cars, private trains, towards their capitals, where they would laugh the deputies, the senators, the congressmen, the M.P.'s out of their chairs, laugh the presidents and the prime ministers, and kaisers and dictators out of their plush-carpeted offices; the sun would wear a broad grin and would whisper the joke to the moon, who would giggle and ripple with it all night long. . . . The red hand of the waiter, with thick nails and work-swollen knuckles, poured Chartreuse into the small glasses before them.

"That," said Tom Randolph, when he had half finished his liqueur, "is the girl for me."

"But, Tom, she's with a French officer."

"They're fighting like cats and dogs. You can see that, can't you?"

"Yes," agreed Howe vaguely.

"Pay the bill. I'll meet you at the corner of the boulevard." Tom Randolph was out of the door. The girl, who had a little of the aspect of a pierrot, with dark skin and bright lips and gold-yellow hat and dress, and the sour-looking officer who was with her, were getting up to go.

At the corner of the boulevard Howe heard a woman's voice joining with Randolph's rich laugh.

"What did I tell you? They split at the door and here we are, Howe. . . . Mademoiselle Montreil, let me introduce a friend. Look, before it's too late, we must have a drink."

At the café table next to them an Englishman was seated with his head sunk on his chest.

"Oh, I say, you woke me up."

"Sorry."

"No harm. Jolly good thing."

They invited him over to their table. There was a moist look about his eyes and a thickness to his voice that denoted alcohol.

"You mustn't mind me. I'm forgetting. . . . I've been doing it for a week. This is the first leave I've had in eighteen months. You Canadians?"

"No. Ambulance service; Americans."

"New at the game then. You're lucky. . . . Before I left the front I saw a man tuck a hand-grenade under the pillow of a poor devil of a German prisoner. The prisoner said, 'Thank you.' The grenade blew him to hell! God! Know anywhere you can get whisky in this bloody town?"

"We'll have to hurry; it's near closing-time."

"Right-o."

They started off, Randolph and the girl talking intimately, their heads close together, Martin supporting the Englishman.

"I need a bit o' whisky to put me on my pins."

They tumbled into the seats round a table at an American bar.

The Englishman felt in his pocket.

"Oh, I say," he cried, "I've got a ticket to the theatre.

It's a box. . . . We can all get in. Come along; let's hurry."

They walked a long while, blundering through the dark streets, and at last stopped at a blue-lighted door.

"Here it is; push in."

"But there are two gentlemen and a lady already in the box, meester."

"No matter, there'll be room." The Englishman waved the ticket in the air.

The little round man with a round red face who was taking the tickets stuttered in bad English and then dropped into French. Meanwhile, the whole party had filed in, leaving the Englishman, who kept waving the ticket in the little man's face.

Two gendarmes, the theatre guards, came up menacingly; the Englishman's face wreathed itself in smiles; he linked an arm in each of the gendarmes', and pushed them towards the bar.

"Come drink to the Entente Cordiale. . . . Vive la France!"

In the box were two Australians and a woman who leaned her head on the chest of one and then the other alternately, laughing so that you could see the gold caps in her black teeth.

They were annoyed at the intrusion that packed the box insupportably tight, so that the woman had to sit on the men's laps, but the air soon cleared in laughter that caused people in the orchestra to stare angrily at the box full of noisy men in khaki. At last the Englishman came, squeezing himself in with a finger mysteriously on his lips. He plucked at Martin's arm, a serious set look coming suddenly over his grey eyes. "It was like this"—his breath laden with whisky was like a halo round Martin's head—"the Hun was a nice little chap, couldn't 'a' been more than eighteen; had a shoulder broken and he thought that my pal was fixing the pillow. He said 'Thank you' with a funny German accent. . . . Mind you, he said 'Thank you'; that's what hurt. And the man laughed. God damn him, he laughed when the poor devil said 'Thank you.' And the grenade blew him to hell."

The stage was a glare of light in Martin's eyes; he felt as he had when at home he had leaned over and looked straight into the headlight of an auto drawn up to the side of the road. Screening him from the glare were the backs of people's heads: Tom Randolph's head and his girl's, side by side, their cheeks touching, the pointed red chin of one of the Australians and the frizzy hair of the other woman.

In the entr'acte they all stood at the bar, where it was very hot and an orchestra was playing and there were many men in khaki in all stages of drunkenness, being led about by women who threw jokes at each other behind the men's backs.

"Here's to mud," said one of the Australians. "The war'll end when everybody is drowned in mud."

The orchestra began playing the *Madelon* and everyone roared out the marching song that, worn threadbare as it was, still had a roistering verve to it that caught people's blood.

People had gone back for the last act. The two Australians, the Englishman, and the two Americans still stood talking.

"Mind you, I'm not what you'd call susceptible. I'm not soft. I got over all that long ago." The Englishman was addressing the company in general. "But the poor beggar said 'Thank you.'"

"What's he saying?" asked a woman, plucking at Martin's arm.

"He's telling about a German atrocity."

"Oh, the dirty Germans! What things they've done!" the woman answered mechanically.

Somehow, during the entr'acte, the Australians had collected another woman; and a strange fat woman with lips painted very small, and very large bulging eyes, had attached herself to Martin. He suffered her because every time he looked at her she burst out laughing.

The bar was closing. They had a drink of champagne all round that made the fat woman give little shrieks of delight. They drifted towards the door, and stood, a formless, irresolute group, in the dark street in front of the theatre.

Randolph came up to Martin.

"Look. We're goin'. I wonder if I ought to leave my money with you . . ."

"I doubt if I'm a safe person to-night. . . ."

"All right. I'll take it along. Look . . . let's meet for breakfast."

"At the *Café de la Paix.*"

"All right. If she is nice I'll bring her."

"She looks charming."

Tom Randolph pressed Martin's hand and was off. There was a sound of a kiss in the darkness.

"I say, I've got to have something to eat," said the Englishman. "I didn't have a bit of dinner. I say—mangai, mangai." He made gestures of putting things into his mouth in the direction of the fat woman.

The three women put their heads together. One of them knew a place, but it was a dreadful place. Really, they mustn't think that. . . . She only knew it because when she was very young a man had taken her there who wanted to seduce her.

At that everyone laughed and the voices of the women rose shrill.

"All right, don't talk; let's go there," said one of the Australians. "We'll attend to the seducing."

A thick woman, a tall comb in the back of her high-piled black hair, and an immovable face with jaw muscled like a prize-fighter's, served them with cold chicken and ham and champagne in a room with mouldering greenish wall-paper lighted by a red-shaded lamp.

The Australians ate and sang and made love to their women. The Englishman went to sleep with his head on the table.

Martin leaned back out of the circle of light, keeping up a desultory conversation with the woman beside him, listening to the sounds of the men's voices down corridors, of the front door being opened and slammed again and again, and of forced, shrill giggles of women.

"Unfortunately, I have an engagement to-night," said Martin to the woman beside him, whose large spherical breasts heaved as she talked, and who rolled herself nearer to him invitingly, seeming with her round pop-eyes and her round cheeks to be made up entirely of small spheres and large soft ones.

"Oh, but it is too late. You can break it."

"It's at four o'clock."

"Then we have time, ducky."

"It's something really romantic, you see."

"The young are always lucky." She rolled her eyes in sympathetic admiration.

"This will be the fourth night this week that I'll sleep without a man. . . . I'll chuck myself into the river soon."

Martin felt himself softening towards her. He slipped a twenty-franc note in her hand.

"Oh, you are too good. You are really galant homme, you."

Martin buried his face in his hands, dreaming of the woman he would like to love to-night. She should be very dark, with red lips and stained cheeks, like Randolph's girl; she should have small breasts and slender, dark, dancer's thighs, and in her arms he could forget everything but the madness and the mystery and the intricate life of Paris about them. He thought of Montmartre, and Louise in the opera standing at her window singing the madness of Paris. . . .

One of the Australians had gone away with a little woman in a pink negligée. The other Australian and the Englishman were standing unsteadily near the table, each supported by a sleepy-looking girl. Leaving the fat woman sadly finishing the remains of the chicken, large tears rolling from her eyes, they left the house and walked for a long time down dark streets, three men and two women, the Englishman being supported in the middle, singing in a desultory fashion.

The girls had two rooms on the fourth floor. As soon as they got there the Englishman tumbled into the bed and went to sleep, snoring loudly.

The Australian took off his coat and opened his shirt. The girls began getting undressed, trying to turn their yawns into little seductive faces.

"Say, old man, have you got a . . ." the Australian whispered in Martin's ear.

"No, I haven't. . . . I'm awfully sorry."

"Never mind. . . . Come along, Janey." He picked his girl up under the arms and, pressing her to him, carried her into the other room.

"Well. . . ." The other girl, in corset and drawers, with her curly brown hair tumbled over one eye and new rouge on her lips, held out her hands. "There's only you and me."

"No, dearie. I must go," said Martin.

"As you will. I'll take care of your friend." She yawned.

He kissed her and stumbled down the dark stairs, his nostrils full of the smell of the rouge on her lips.

He walked a long while with his hat off, breathing deep of the sharp night air. The streets were black and silent. Intemperate desires prowled about him like cats in the darkness.

He woke up and stretched himself stiffly, smelling grass and damp earth. A pearly lavender mist was all about him, through which loomed the square towers of Notre Dame and the row of kings across the façade and the sculpture about the darkness of the doorways. He had lain down on his back on the little grass plot of the Parvis Notre Dame to look at the stars, and had fallen asleep.

It must be nearly dawn. Words were droning importunately in his head. "The poor beggar said 'Thank you' with a funny German accent and the grenade blew him to hell." He remembered the man he had once helped to pick up in whose pocket a grenade had exploded. Before that he had not realized that torn flesh was such a black red, like sausage meat.

"Get up, you can't lie there," cried a gendarme.

"Notre Dame is beautiful in the morning," said Martin, stepping across the low rail on to the pavement.

"Ah, yes; it is beautiful."

Martin Howe sat on the rail of the bridge and looked. Before him, with nothing distinct yet to be seen, were two square towers and the tracery between them and the row of kings on the façade, and the long series of flying buttresses of the flank, gleaming through the mist, and, barely visible, the dark, slender spire soaring above the crossing. So had the abbey in the forest gleamed tall in the misty moonlight; like mist, only drab and dense, the dust had risen above the tall apse as the shells tore it to pieces.

Amid a smell of new-roasted coffee he sat at a table and watched people pass briskly through the ruddy sunlight. Waiters in shirt-sleeves were rubbing off the other tables and putting out the chairs. He sat sipping coffee, feeling languid and nerveless. After a while Tom Randolph, looking very young and brown with his hat a little on one side, came along. With him, plainly dressed in blue serge, was the girl. They sat down and she dropped her head on his shoulder, covering her eyes with her dark lashes.

"Oh, I am so tired."

"Poor child! You must go home and go back to bed."

"But I've got to go to work."

"Poor thing." They kissed each other tenderly and languidly.

The waiter came with coffee and hot milk and little crisp loaves of bread.

"Oh, Paris is wonderful in the early morning!" said Martin.

"Indeed it is. . . . Good-bye, little girl, if you must go. We'll see each other again."

"You must call me Yvonne." She pouted a little.

"All right, Yvonne." He got to his feet and pressed her two hands.

"Well, what sort of a time did you have, Howe?"

"Curious. I lost our friends one by one, left two women and slept a little while on the grass in front of Notre Dame. That was my real love of the night."

"My girl was charming. . . . Honestly, I'd marry her in a minute." He laughed a merry laugh.

"Let's take a cab somewhere."

They climbed into a victoria and told the driver to go to the Madeleine.

"Look, before I do anything else I must go to the hotel."

"Why?"

"Preventives."

"Of course; you'd better go at once."

The cab rattled merrily along the streets where the early sunshine cast rusty patches on the grey houses and on the thronged fantastic chimney-pots that rose in clusters and hedges from the mansard roofs.

Chapter VI

THE lamp in the hut of the road control casts an oblong of light on the white wall opposite. The patch of light is constantly crossed and scalloped and obscured by shadows of rifles and helmets and packs of men passing. Now and then the shadow of a single man, a nose and a chin under a helmet, a head bent forward with the weight of the pack, or a pack alone beside which slants a rifle, shows up huge and fantastic with its loaf of bread and its pair of shoes and its pots and pans.

Then with a jingle of harness and clank of steel, train after train of artillery comes up out of the darkness of the road, is thrown by the lamp into vivid relief and is swallowed again by the blackness of the village street, short bodies of seventy-fives sticking like ducks' tails from between their large wheels; caisson after caisson of ammunition, huge waggons hooded and unhooded, filled with a chaos of equipment that catches fantastic lights and throws huge muddled shadows on the white wall of the house.

"Put that light out. Name of God, do you want to

have them start chucking shells into here?" comes a voice shrill with anger. The brisk trot of the officer's horse is lost in the clangour.

The door of the hut slams to and only a thin ray of orange light penetrates into the blackness of the road, where with jingle of harness and clatter of iron and tramp of hoofs, gun after gun, caisson after caisson, waggon after waggon files by. Now and then the passing stops entirely and matches flare where men light pipes and cigarettes. Coming from the other direction with throbbing of motors, a convoy of camions, huge black oblongs, grinds down the other side of the road. Horses rear and there are shouts and curses and clacking of reins in the darkness.

Far away where the lowering clouds meet the hills beyond the village a white glare grows and fades again at intervals: star-shells.

"There's a most tremendous concentration of sanitary sections."

"You bet; two American sections and a French one in this village; three more down the road. Something's up."

"There's goin' to be an attack at St. Mihiel, a Frenchman told me."

"I heard that the Germans were concentrating for an offensive in the Four de Paris."

"Damned unlikely."

"Anyway, this is the third week we've been in this bloody hold with our feet in the mud."

"They've got us quartered in a barn with a regular brook flowing through the middle of it."

"The main thing about this damned war is ennui— just plain boredom."

"Not forgetting the mud."

Three ambulance drivers in slickers were on the front seat of a car. The rain fell in perpendicular sheets, pattering on the roof of the car and on the puddles that filled the village street. Streaming with water, blackened walls of ruined houses rose opposite them above a rank growth of weeds. Beyond were rain-veiled hills. Every little while, slithering through the rain, splashing mud to the right and left, a convoy of camions went by and disappeared, truck after truck, in the white streaming rain.

Inside the car Tom Randolph was playing an accordion, letting strange nostalgic little songs filter out amid the hard patter of the rain.

"Oh, I's been workin' on de railroad
All de livelong day;
I's been workin' on de railroad
Jus' to pass de time away."

The men on the front seat leaned back and shook the water off their knees and hummed the song.

The accordion had stopped. Tom Randolph was

lying on his back on the floor of the car with his arm over his eyes. The rain fell endlessly, rattling on the roof of the car, dancing silver in the coffee-coloured puddles of the road. Their boredom fell into the rhythm of crooning self-pity of the old coon song:

> *"I's been workin' on de railroad*
> *All de livelong day;*
> *I's been workin' on de railroad*
> *Jus' to pass de time away."*

"Oh, God, something's got to happen soon."

Lost in rubber boots, and a huge gleaming slicker and hood, the section leader splashed across the road.

"All cars must be ready to leave at six to-night."

"Yay. Where we goin'?"

"Orders haven't come yet. We're to be in readiness to leave at six to-night. . . ."

"I tell you, fellers, there's goin' to be an attack. This concentration of sanitary sections means something. You can't tell me . . ."

"They say they have beer," said the aspirant behind Martin in the long line of men who waited in the hot sun for the copé to open, while the dust the staff cars and camions raised as they whirred by on the road settled in a blanket over the village.

"Cold beer?"

"Of course not," said the aspirant, laughing so that all

the brilliant ivory teeth showed behind his red lips. "It'll be detestable. I'm getting it because it's rare, for sentimental reasons."

Martin laughed, looking in the man's brown face, a face in which all past expressions seemed to linger in the fine lines about the mouth and eyes and in the modelling of the cheeks and temples.

"You don't understand that," said the aspirant again.

"Indeed I do."

Later they sat on the edge of the stone well-head in the courtyard behind the store, drinking warm beer out of tin cups blackened by wine, and staring at a tall barn that had crumpled at one end so that it looked, with its two frightened little square windows, like a cow kneeling down.

"Is it true that the ninety-second's going up to the lines to-night?"

"Yes, we're going up to make a little attack. Probably I'll come back in your little omnibus."

"I hope you won't."

"I'd be very glad to. A lucky wound! But I'll probably be killed. This is the first time I've gone up to the front that I didn't expect to be killed. So it'll probably happen."

Martin Howe could not help looking at him suddenly. The aspirant sat at ease on the stone margin of the well, leaning against the wrought iron support for the bucket, one knee clasped in his strong, heavilyveined hands. Dead he would be different. Martin's mind could hardly grasp the connection between this man full of latent energies, full of thoughts and desires, this man whose shoulder he would have liked to have put his arm round from friendliness, with whom he would have liked to go for long walks, with whom he would have liked to sit long into the night drinking and talking—and those huddled, pulpy masses of blue uniform half-buried in the mud of ditches.

"Have you ever seen a herd of cattle being driven to abattoir on a fine May morning?" asked the aspirant in a scornful, jaunty tone, as if he had guessed Martin's thoughts.

"I wonder what they think of it."

"It's not that I'm resigned. . . . Don't think that. Resignation is too easy. That's why the herd can be driven by a boy of six . . . or a prime minister!"

Martin was sitting with his arms crossed. The fingers of one hand were squeezing the muscle of his forearm. It gave him pleasure to feel the smooth, firm modelling of his arm through his sleeve. And how would that feel when it was dead, when a steel splinter had slithered through it? A momentary stench of putrefaction filled his nostrils, making his stomach contract with nausea.

"I'm not resigned either," he shouted in a laugh. "I am going to do something some day, but first I must see. I want to be initiated in all the circles of hell."

"I'd play the part of Virgil pretty well," said the aspirant, "but I suppose Virgil was a staff officer."

"I must go," said Martin. "My name's Martin Howe, S.S.U. 84."

"Oh yes, you are quartered in the square. My name is Merrier. You'll probably carry me back in your little omnibus."

When Howe got back to where the cars were packed in a row in the village square, Randolph came up to him and whispered in his ear:

"D.J.'s to-morrow."

"What's that?"

"The attack. It's to-morrow at three in the morning; instructions are going to be given out to-night."

A detonation behind them was a blow on the head, making their ear-drums ring. The glass in the headlight of one of the cars tinkled to the ground.

"The 410 behind the church, that was. Pretty near knocks the wind out of you."

"Say, Randolph, have you heard the new orders?"

"No."

A tall, fair-haired man came out from the front of his car where he had been working on the motor, holding his grease-covered hands away from him.

"It's put off," he said, lowering his voice mysteriously. "D.J.'s not till day after to-morrow at four-twenty. But to-morrow we're going up to relieve the section that's coming out and take over the posts. They say it's hell up there. The Germans have a new gas that you can't smell at all. The other section's got about five men gassed, and a bunch of them have broken down. The posts are shelled all the time."

"Great," said Tom Randolph. "We'll see the real thing this time."

There was a whistling shriek overhead and all three of them fell in a heap on the ground in front of the car. There was a crash that echoed amid the house-walls, and a pillar of black smoke stood like a cypress tree at the other end of the village street.

"Talk about the real thing!" said Martin.

"Ole 410 evidently woke 'em up some."

It was the fifth time that day that Martin's car had passed the cross-roads where the calvary was. Someone had propped up the fallen crucifix so that it tilted dark despairing arms against the sunset sky where the sun gleamed like a huge copper kettle lost in its own steam. The rain made bright yellowish stripes across the sky and dripped from the cracked feet of the old wooden Christ, whose gaunt, scarred figure hung out from the tilted cross, swaying a little under the beating of the rain. Martin was wiping the mud from his hands after changing a wheel. He stared curiously at the fallen jowl and the cavernous eyes that had meant for some country sculptor ages ago the utterest agony of pain. Suddenly he noticed that where the crown of thorns had been about the forehead of the Christ someone had wound barbed wire. He smiled, asking the swaying figure in his mind, "What do You think of it, old boy? How do You like Your followers? Not so romantic as thorns, is it, that barbed wire?"

He leaned over to crank the car.

The road was filled suddenly with the tramp and splash of troops marching, their wet helmets and their rifles gleaming in the coppery sunset. Even through the clean rain came the smell of filth and sweat and misery of troops marching. The faces under the helmets were strained and colourless and cadaverous from the weight of the equipment on their necks and their backs and their thighs. The faces drooped under the helmets, tilted to one side or the other, distorted and wooden like the face of the figure that dangled from the cross.

Above the splash of feet through mud and the jingle of equipment, came occasionally the ping, ping of shrapnel bursting at the next cross-roads at the edge of the woods.

Martin sat in the car with the motor racing, waiting for the end of the column.

One of the stragglers who floundered along through the churned mud of the road after the regular ranks had passed stopped still and looked up at the tilted cross. From the next cross-roads came, at intervals, the sharp twanging ping of shrapnel bursting.

The straggler suddenly began kicking feebly at the prop of the cross with his foot, and then dragged himself off after the column. The cross fell forward with a dull splintering splash into the mud of the road.

The road went down the hill in long zig-zags, through a village at the bottom where out of the mist that steamed from the little river a spire with a bent weathercock rose above the broken roof of the church, then up the hill again into the woods. In the woods the road stretched green and gold in the first horizontal sunlight. Among the thick trees, roofs covered with branches, were rows of long portable barracks with doors decorated with rustic work. At one place a sign announced in letters made of wattled sticks, *Camp des Pommiers*.

A few birds sang in the woods, and at a pump they passed a lot of men stripped to the waist who were leaning over washing, laughing and splashing in the sunlight. Every now and then, distant, metallic, the pong, pong, pong of a battery of seventy-fives resounded through the rustling trees.

"Looks like a camp meetin' ground in Georgia," said Tom Randolph, blowing his whistle to make two men carrying a large steaming pot on a pole between them get out of the way.

The road became muddier as they went deeper into the woods, and, turning into a cross-road, the car began slithering, skidding a little at the turns, through thick soupy mud. On either side the woods became broken and jagged, stumps and split boughs littering the ground, trees snapped off halfway up. In the air there was a scent of newly-split timber and of turned-up woodland earth, and among them a sweetish rough smell.

Covered with greenish mud, splashing the mud right and left with their great flat wheels, camions began passing them returning from the direction of the lines.

At last at a small red cross flag they stopped and ran the car into a grove of tall chestnuts, where they parked it beside another car of their section and lay down among the crisp leaves, listening to occasional shells whining far overhead. All through the wood was a continuous ping, pong, ping of batteries, with the crash of a big gun coming now and then like the growl of a bullfrog among the sing-song of small toads in a pond at night.

Through the trees from which they lay they could see the close-packed wooden crosses of a cemetery from which came a sound of spaded earth, and where, preceded by a priest in a muddy cassock, little two-wheeled carts piled with shapeless things in sacks kept being brought up and unloaded and dragged away again.

Showing alternately dark and light in the sun and shadow of the woodland road, a cook waggon, short chimney giving out blue smoke, and cauldrons steaming, clatters ahead of Martin and Randolph; the backs of two men in heavy blue coats, their helmets showing above the narrow driver's seat. On either side of the road short yellow flames keep spitting up, slanting from hidden guns amid a pandemonium of noise.

Up the road a sudden column of black smoke rises among falling trees. A louder explosion and the cook waggon in front of them vanishes in a new whirl of thick smoke. Accelerator pressed down, the car plunges along the rutted road, tips, and a wheel sinks in the new shell-hole. The hind wheels spin for a moment, spattering gravel about, and just as another roar comes behind them, bite into the road again and the car goes on, speeding through the alternate sun and shadow of the woods. Martin remembers the beating legs of a mule rolling on its back on the side of the road and, steaming in the fresh morning air, the purple and yellow and red of its ripped belly.

"Did you get the smell of almonds? I sort of like it," says Randolph, drawing a long breath as the car slowed down again.

The woods at night, fantastic blackness full of noise and yellow leaping flames from the mouths of guns. Now and then the sulphurous flash of a shell explosion and the sound of trees falling and shell fragments swishing through the air. At intervals over a little knoll in the direction of the trenches, a white star-shell falls slowly, making the trees and the guns among their tangle of hiding branches cast long green-black shadows, drowning the wood in a strange glare of desolation.

"Where the devil's the abri?"

Everything drowned in the detonations of three guns, one after the other, so near as to puff hot air in their faces in the midst of the blinding concussion.

"Look, Tom, this is foolish; the abri's right here."

"I haven't got it in my pocket, Howe. Damn those guns."

Again everything is crushed in the concussion of the guns.

They throw themselves on the ground as a shell shrieks and explodes. There is a moment's pause, and gravel and bits of bark tumble about their heads.

"We've got to find that abri. I wish I hadn't lost my flashlight."

"Here it is! No, that stinks too much. Must be the latrine."

"Say, Tom."

"Here."

"Damn, I ran into a tree. I found it."

"All right. Coming."

Martin held out his hand until Randolph bumped into it; then they stumbled together down the rough wooden steps, pulled aside the blanket that served to keep the light in, and found themselves blinking in the low tunnel of the abri.

Brancardiers were asleep in the two tiers of bunks that filled up the sides, and at the table at the end a lieutenant of the medical corps was writing by the light of a smoky lamp.

"They are landing some round here to-night," he said, pointing out two unoccupied bunks. "I'll call you when we need a car."

As he spoke, in succession the three big guns went off. The concussion put the lamp out.

"Damn," said Tom Randolph.

The lieutenant swore and struck a match.

"The red light of the poste de secours is out, too," said Martin.

"No use lighting it again with those unholy mortars. . . . It's idiotic to put a poste de secours in the middle of a battery like this."

The Americans lay down to try to sleep. Shell after shell exploded round the dugout, but regularly every few minutes came the hammer blows of the mortars, half the time putting the light out.

A shell explosion seemed to split the dugout and a piece of éclat whizzed through the blanket that curtained off the door. Someone tried to pick it up as it lay half-buried in the board floor, and pulled his fingers away quickly, blowing on them. The men turned over in the bunks and laughed, and a smile came over the drawn green face of a wounded man who sat very quiet behind the lieutenant, staring at the smoky flame of the lamp.

The curtain was pulled aside and a man staggered in holding with the other hand a limp arm twisted in a mud-covered sleeve, from which blood and mud dripped on to the floor.

"Hello, old chap," said the doctor quietly. A smell of disinfectant stole through the dugout.

Faint above the incessant throbbing of explosions the sound of a claxon horn.

"Ha, gas," said the doctor. "Put on your masks, children." A man went along the dugout waking those who were asleep and giving out fresh masks. Someone stood in the doorway blowing a shrill whistle, then there was again the clamour of a claxon near at hand.

The band of the gas-mask was tight about Martin's forehead, biting into the skin.

He and Randolph sat side by side on the edge of the bunk, looking out through the crinkled isinglass eye-pieces at the men in the dugout, most of whom had gone to sleep again.

"God, I envy a man who can snore through a gas-mask," said Randolph.

Men's heads had a ghoulish look, strange large eyes and grey oilcloth flaps instead of faces.

Outside the constant explosions had given place to a series of swishing whistles, merging together into a sound as of water falling, only less regular, more sibilant. Occasionally there was the rending burst of a shell, and at intervals came the swinging detonations of the three guns. In the dugout, except for two men who snored loudly, raspingly, everyone was quiet.

Several stretchers with wounded men on them were brought in and laid in the end of the dugout.

Gradually, as the bombardment continued, men began sliding into the dugout, crowding together, touching each other for company, speaking in low voices through their masks.

"A mask, in the name of God, a mask!" a voice shouted, breaking into a squeal, and an unshaven man, with mud caked in his hair and beard, burst through the curtain. His eyelids kept up a continual trembling and the water streamed down both sides of his nose.

"O God," he kept talking in a rasping whisper, "O God, they're all killed. There were six mules on my waggon and a shell killed them all and threw me into the ditch. You can't find the road any more. They're all killed."

An orderly was wiping his face as if it were a child's.

"They're all killed and I lost my mask. . . . O God, this gas . . ."

The doctor, a short man, looking like a gnome in his mask with its wheezing rubber nosepiece, was walking up and down with short, slow steps.

Suddenly, as three soldiers came in drawing the curtain aside, he shouted in a shrill, high-pitched voice:

"Keep the curtain closed! Do you want to asphyxiate us?"

He strode up to the newcomers, his voice strident like an angry woman's. "What are you doing here? This is the poste de secours. Are you wounded?"

"But, my lieutenant, we can't stay outside . . ."

"Where's your own cantonment? You can't stay here; you can't stay here," he shrieked.

"But, my lieutenant, our dugout's been hit."

"You can't stay here. You can't stay here. There's not enough room for the wounded. Name of God!"

"But, my lieutenant . . ."

"Get the hell out of here, d'you hear?"

The men began stumbling out into the darkness, tightening the adjustments of their masks behind their heads.

The guns had stopped firing. There was nothing but the constant swishing and whistling of gas-shells, like endless pails of dirty water being thrown on gravel.

"We've been at it three hours," whispered Martin to Tom Randolph.

"God, suppose these masks need changing."

The sweat from Martin's face steamed in the eye-pieces, blinding him.

"Any more masks?" he asked.

A brancardier handed him one. "There aren't any more in the abri."

"I have some more in the car," said Martin.

"I'll get one," cried Randolph, getting to his feet.

They started out of the door together. In the light that streamed out as they drew the flap aside they saw a tree opposite them. A shell exploded, it seemed, right on top of them; the tree rose and bowed towards them and fell.

"Are you all there, Tom?" whispered Martin, his ears ringing.

"Bet your life."

Someone pulled them back into the abri. "Here; we've found another."

Martin lay down on the bunk again, drawing with difficulty each breath. His lips had a wet, decomposed feeling.

At the wrist of the arm he rested his head on, the watch ticked comfortably.

He began to think how ridiculous it would be if he, Martin Howe, should be extinguished like this. The gas-mask might be defective.

God, it would be silly.

Outside the gas-shells were still coming in. The lamp showed through a faint bluish haze. Everyone was still waiting.

Another hour.

Martin began to recite to himself the only thing he

could remember, over and over again in time to the ticking of his watch.

> "*Ah, sunflower, weary of time.*
> *Ah, sunflower, weary of time,*
> *Who countest the steps of the sun;*
> *Ah, sunflower, weary of time,*
> *Who countest . . ."*

"One, two, three, four," he counted the shells outside exploding at irregular intervals.

There were periods of absolute silence, when he could hear batteries pong, pong, pong in the distance.

He began again.

> "*Ah, sunflower, weary of time,*
> *Who countest the steps of the sun*
> *In search of that far golden clime*
> *Where the traveller's journey is done.*

> "*Where the youth pined away with desire*
> *And the pale virgin shrouded in snow*
> *Arise from their graves and aspire*
> *Where my sunflower wishes to go."*

Whang, whang, whang; the battery alongside began again, sending out the light. Someone pulled the blanket aside. A little leprous greyness filtered into the dugout.

"Ah, it's getting light."

The doctor went out and they could hear his steps climbing up to the level of the ground.

Howe saw a man take his mask off and spit.

"O God, a cigarette!" Tom Randolph cried, pulling his mask off. The air of the woods was fresh and cool outside. Everything was lost in mist that filled the shell-holes as with water and wreathed itself fantastically about the shattered trunks of trees. Here and there was still a little greenish haze of gas. It cut their throats and made their eyes run as they breathed in the cool air of the dawn.

Dawn in a wilderness of jagged stumps and ploughed earth; against the yellow sky, the yellow glare of guns that squat like toads in a tangle of wire and piles of brass shell-cases and split wooden boxes. Long rutted roads littered with shell-cases stretching through the wrecked woods in the yellow light; strung alongside of them, tangled masses of telephone wires. Torn camouflage fluttering greenish-grey against the ardent yellow sky, and twining among the fantastic black leafless trees, the greenish wraiths of gas. Along the roads camions over-turned, dead mules tangled in their traces beside shattered caissons, huddled bodies in long blue coats half buried in the mud of the ditches.

"We've got to pass. . . . We've got five very bad cases."

"Impossible."

"We've got to pass. . . . Sacred name of God!"

"But it is impossible. Two camions are blocked across

the road and there are three batteries of seventy-fives waiting to get up the road."

Long lines of men on horseback with gas-masks on, a rearing of frightened horses and jingle of harness.

"Talk to 'em, Howe, for God's sake; we've got to get past."

"I'm doing the best I can, Tom."

"Well, make 'em look lively. Damn this gas!"

"Put your masks on again; you can't breathe without them in this hollow."

"Hay! ye God-damn sons of bitches, get out of the way."

"But they can't."

"Oh, hell, I'll go talk to 'em. You take the wheel."

"No, sit still and don't get excited."

"You're the one's getting excited."

"Damn this gas."

"My lieutenant, I beg you to move the horses to the side of the road. I have five very badly wounded men. They will die in this gas. I've got to get by."

"God damn him, tell him to hurry."

"Shut up, Tom, for God's sake."

"They're moving. I can't see a thing in this mask."

"Hah, that did for the two back horses."

"Halt! Is there any room in the ambulance? One of my men's just got his thigh ripped up."

"No room, no room."

"He'll have to go to a poste de secours."

The fresh air blowing hard in their faces and the woods getting greener on either side, full of ferns and small plants that half cover the strands of barbed wire and the rows of shells.

At the end of the woods the sun rises golden into a cloudless sky, and on the grassy slope of the valley sheep and a herd of little donkeys are feeding, looking up with quietly moving jaws as the ambulance, smelling of blood and filthy sweat-soaked clothes, rattles by.

Black night. All through the woods along the road squatting mortars spit yellow flame. Constant throbbing of detonations.

Martin, inside the ambulance, is holding together a broken stretcher, while the car jolts slowly along. It is pitch dark in the car, except when the glare of a gun from near the road gives him a momentary view of the man's head, a mass of bandages from the middle of which a little bit of blood-soaked beard sticks out, and of his lean body tossing on the stretcher with every jolt of the car. Martin is kneeling on the floor of the car, his knees bruised by the jolting, holding the man on the stretcher, with his chest pressed on the man's chest and one arm stretched down to keep the limp bandaged leg still.

The man's breath comes with a bubbling sound, now and then mingling with an articulate groan.

"Softly. . . . Oh, softly, oh—oh—oh!"

"Slow as you can, Tom, old man," Martin calls out above the pandemonium of firing on both sides of the road, tightening the muscles of his arm in a desperate effort to keep the limp leg from bouncing. The smell of blood and filth is misery in his nostrils.

"Softly. . . . Softly. . . . Oh—oh—oh!" The groan is barely heard amid the bubbling breath.

Pitch dark in the car. Martin, his every muscle taut with the agony of the man's pain, is on his knees, pressing his chest on the man's chest, trying with an arm stretched along the man's leg to keep him from bouncing in the broken stretcher.

"Needn't have troubled to have brought him," said the hospital orderly, as blood dripped fast from the stretcher, black in the light of the lantern. "He's pretty near dead now. He won't last long."

Chapter VII

So you like it, Will? You like this sort of thing?"
Martin Howe was stretched on the grass of a hillside a little above a cross-roads. Beside him squatted a
ruddy-faced youth with a smudge of grease on his
faintly-hooked nose. A champagne bottle rested against
his knees.

"Yes. I've never been happier in my life. It's a coarse
boozing sort of a life, but I like it."

They looked over the landscape of greyish rolling
hills scarred everywhere by new roads and ranks of
wooden shacks. Along the road beneath them crawled
like beetles convoy after convoy of motor trucks. The
wind came to them full of a stench of latrines and of the
exhaust of motors.

"The last time I saw you," said Martin, after a pause,
"was early one morning on the Cambridge bridge. I was
walking out from Boston, and we talked of the Eroica
they'd played at the Symphony, and you said it was
silly to have a great musician try to play soldier. D'you
remember?"

"No. That was in another incarnation. Have some fizz."

He poured from the bottle into a battered tin cup.

"But talking about playing soldier, Howe, I must tell you about how our lieutenant got the Croix de Guerre. . . . Somebody ought to write a book called *Heroisms of the Great War.* . . ."

"I am sure that many people have, and will. You probably'll do it yourself, Will. But go on."

The sun burst from the huddled clouds for a moment, mottling the hills and the scarred valleys with light. The shadow of an aeroplane flying low passed across the field, and the snoring of its motors cut out all other sound.

"Well, our louie's name's Duval, but he spells it with a small 'd' and a big 'V.' He's been wanting a Croix de Guerre for a hell of a time because lots of fellows in the section have been getting 'em. He tried giving dinners to the General Staff and everything, but that didn't seem to work. So there was nothing to it but to get wounded. So he took to going to the front posts; but the trouble was that it was a hell of a quiet sector and no shells ever came within a mile of it. At last somebody made a mistake and a little Austrian eighty-eight came tumbling in and popped about fifty yards from his staff car. He showed the most marvellous presence of mind, 'cause he clapped his hand over his eye and sank back in the seat with a groan. The doctor asked what was the matter, but old Duval just kept his hand tight over his eye and said, 'Nothing, nothing; just a scratch,' and went off to inspect the posts. Of course the posts didn't need inspecting. And he rode round all day with a hand-kerchief over one eye and a look of heroism in the other. But never would he let the doctor even peep at it. Next morning he came out with a bandage round his head as big as a sheik's turban. He went to see headquar-ters in that get-up and lunched with the staff-officers. Well, he got his Croix de Guerre all right—cited for assuring the evacuation of the wounded under fire and all the rest of it."

"Some bird. He'll probably get to be a general before the war's over."

Howe poured out the last of the champagne, and threw the bottle listlessly off into the grass, where it struck an empty shell-case and broke.

"But, Will, you can't like this," he said. "It's all so like an ash-heap, a huge garbage-dump of men and equipment."

"I suppose it is . . ." said the ruddy-faced youth, dis-covering the grease on his nose and rubbing it off with the back of his hand.

"Damn those dirty Fords. They get grease all over you! I suppose it is that life was so dull in America that anything seems better. I worked a year in an office be-fore leaving home. Give me the garbage-dump."

"Look," said Martin, shading his eyes with his hand

and staring straight up into the sky. "There are two planes fighting."

They both screwed up their eyes to stare into the sky, where two bits of mica were circling. Below them, like wads of cotton-wool, some white and others black, were rows of the smoke-puffs of shrapnel from anti-aircraft guns.

The two boys watched the specks in silence. At last one began to grow larger, seemed to be falling in wide spirals. The other had vanished. The falling aeroplane started rising again into the middle sky, then stopped suddenly, burst into flames, and fluttered down behind the hills, leaving an irregular trail of smoke.

"More garbage," said the ruddy-faced youth, as he rose to his feet.

"Shrapnel. What a funny place to shoot shrapnel!"

"They must have got the bead on that bunch of material the genie's bringing in."

There was an explosion and a vicious whine of shrapnel bullets among the trees. On the road a staff-car turned round hastily and speeded back.

Martin got up from where he was lying on the grass under a pine tree, looking at the sky, and put his helmet on; as he did so there was another sharp bang overhead and a little reddish-brown cloud that suddenly spread and drifted away among the quiet tree-tops. He took off his helmet and examined it quizzically.

"Tom, I've got a dent in the helmet."

Tom Randolph made a grab for the little piece of jagged iron that had rebounded from the helmet and lay at his feet.

"God damn, it's hot," he cried, dropping it; "anyway, finding's keepings." He put his foot on the shrapnel splinter.

"That ought to be mine, I swear, Tom."

"You've got the dent, Howe; what more do you want?"

"Damn hog."

Martin sat on the top step of the dugout, diving down whenever he heard a shell-shriek loudening in the distance. Beside him was a tall man with the crossed cannon of the artillery in his helmet, and a shrunken brown face with crimson-veined checks and very long silky black moustaches.

"A dirty business," he said. "It's idiotic. . . . Name of a dog!"

Grabbing each other's arms, they tumbled down the steps together as a shell passed overhead to burst in a tree down the road.

"Now look at that." The man held up his musette to Howe. "I've broken the bottle of Bordeaux I had in my musette. It's idiotic."

"Been on permission?"

"Don't I look it?"

They sat at the top of the steps again; the man took

out bits of wet glass dripping red wine from his little bag, swearing all the while.

"I was bringing it to the little captain. He's a nice little old chap, the little captain, and he loves good wine."

"Bordeaux?"

"Can't you smell it? It's Medoc, 1900, from my own vines. . . . Look, taste it, there's still a little." He held up the neck of the bottle and Martin took a sip.

The artilleryman drank the rest of it, twisted his long moustaches and heaved a deep sigh.

"Go there, my poor good old wine." He threw the remnants of the bottle into the underbrush. Shrapnel burst a little down the road. "Oh, this is a dirty business! I am a Gascon. . . . I like to live." He put a dirty brown hand on Martin's arm.

"How old do you think I am?"

"Thirty-five."

"I am twenty-four. Look at the picture." From a tattered black note-book held together by an elastic band he pulled a snapshot of a jolly-looking young man with a fleshy face and his hands tucked into the top of a wide, tightly-wound sash. He looked at the picture, smiling and tugging at one of his long moustaches. "Then I was twenty. It's the war." He shrugged his shoulders and put the picture carefully back into his inside pocket. "Oh, it's idiotic!"

"You must have had a tough time."

"It's just that people aren't meant for this sort of

thing," said the artilleryman quietly. "You don't get accustomed. The more you see the worse it is. Then you end by going crazy. Oh, it's idiotic!"

"How did you find things at home?"

"Oh, at home! Oh, what do I care about that now? They get on without you. . . . But we used to know how to live, we Gascons. We worked so hard on the vines and on the fruit-trees, and we kept a horse and carriage. I had the best-looking rig in the department. Sunday it was fun; we'd play bowls and I'd ride about with my wife. Oh, she was nice in those days! She was young and fat and laughed all the time. She was something a man could put his arms around, she was. We'd go out in my rig. It was click-clack of the whip in the air and off we were in the broad road. . . . Sacred name of a pig, that one was close. . . . And the Marquis of Montmarieul had a rig, too, but not so good as mine, and my horse would always pass his in the road. Oh, it was funny, and he'd look so sour to have common people like us pass him in the road. . . . Boom, there's another. . . . And the Marquis now is nicely embusqué in the automobile service. He is stationed at Versailles. . . . And look at me. . . . But what do I care about all that now?"

"But after the war . . ."

"After the war?" He spat savagely on the first step of the dugout. "They learn to get on without you."

"But we'll be free to do as we please."

"We'll never forget."

"I shall go to Spain . . ." A piece of shrapnel ripped past Martin's ear, cutting off the sentence.

"Name of God! It's getting hot. . . . Spain: I know Spain." The artilleryman jumped up and began dancing, Spanish fashion, snapping his fingers, his big moustaches swaying and trembling. Several shells burst down the road in quick succession, filling the air with a whine of fragments.

"A cook waggon got it!" the artilleryman shouted, dancing on. "Tra-la la la-la-la-la, la-la la," he sang, snapping his fingers.

He stopped and spat again.

"What do I care?" he said. "Well, so long, old chap. I must go. . . . Say, let's change knives—a little souvenir."

"Great."

"Good luck."

The artilleryman strode off through the woods, past the portable fence that surrounded the huddled wooden crosses of the graveyard.

Against the red glare of the dawn the wilderness of shattered trees stands out purple, hidden by grey mist in the hollows, looped and draped fantastically with strands of telephone wire and barbed wire, tangled like leafless creepers, that hang in clots against the red sky. Here and there guns squat among piles of shells covered with mottled green cheese-cloth, and spit long tongues of yellow flame against the sky. The ambulance waits by the side of the rutted road littered with tin cans and brass shell-cases, while a doctor and two stretcher-bearers bend over a man on a stretcher laid among the underbrush. The man groans and there is a sound of ripping bandages. On the other side of the road a fallen mule feebly wags its head from side to side, a mass of purple froth hanging from its mouth and wide-stretched scarlet nostrils.

There is a new smell in the wind, a smell unutterably sordid, like the smell of the poor immigrants landing at Ellis Island. Martin Howe glances round and sees advancing down the road ranks and ranks of strange grey men whose mushroom-shaped helmets give an eerie look as of men from the moon in a fairy tale.

"Why, they're Germans," he says to himself; "I'd quite forgotten they existed."

"Ah, they're prisoners." The doctor gets to his feet and glances down the road and then turns to his work again.

The tramp of feet marching in unison on the rough shell-pitted road, and piles and piles of grey men clotted with dried mud, from whom comes the new smell, the sordid, miserable smell of the enemy.

"Things going well?" Martin asks a guard, a man with ashen face and eyes that burn out of black sockets.

"How should I know?"

"Many prisoners?"

"How should I know?"

The captain and the aumonier are taking their breakfast, each sitting on a packing-box with their tin cups and tin plates ranged on the board propped up between them. All round red clay, out of which the abri was excavated. A smell of antiseptics from the door of the dressing-station and of lime and latrines mingling with the greasy smell of the movable kitchen not far away. They are eating dessert, slices of pineapple speared with a knife out of a can. In their manner there is something that makes Martin see vividly two gentlemen in frock-coats dining at a table under the awning of a café on the boulevards. It has a leisurely ceremoniousness, an ease that could exist nowhere else.

"No, my friend," the doctor is saying, "I do not think that an apprehension of religion existed in the mind of palæolithic man."

"But, my captain, don't you think that you scientific people sometimes lose a little of the significance of things, insisting always on their scientific, in this case on their anthropological, aspect?"

"Not in the least; it is the only way to look at them."

"There are other ways," says the aumonier, smiling.

"One moment. . . ." From under the packing-box the captain produced a small bottle of anisette. "You'll have a little glass, won't you?"

"With the greatest pleasure. What a rarity here, anisette."

"But, as I was about to say, take our life here, for an example." . . . A shell shrieks overhead and crashes hollowly in the woods behind the dugout. Another follows it, exploding nearer. The captain picks a few bits of gravel off the table, reaches for his helmet and continues. "For example, our life here, which is, as was the life of palæolithic man, taken up only with the bare struggle for existence against overwhelming odds. You know yourself that it is not conducive to religion or any emotion except that of preservation."

"I hardly admit that. . . . Ah, I saved it," the aumonier announces, catching the bottle of anisette as it is about to fall off the table. An exploding shell rends the air about them. There is a pause, and a shower of earth and gravel tumbles about their ears.

"I must go and see if anyone was hurt," says the aumonier, clambering up the clay bank to the level of the ground; "but you will admit, my captain, that the sentiment of preservation is at least akin to the fundamental feelings of religion."

"My dear friend, I admit nothing. . . . Till this evening, good-bye." He waves his hand and goes into the dugout.

Martin and two French soldiers drinking sour wine in the doorway of a deserted house. It was raining outside and now and then a dripping camion passed along the road, slithering through the mud.

"This is the last summer of the war. . . . It must be," said the little man with large brown eyes and a childish, chubby brown face, who sat on Martin's left.

"Why?"

"Oh, I don't know. Everyone feels like that."

"I don't see," said Martin, "why it shouldn't last for ten or twenty years. Wars have before. . . ."

"How long have you been at the front?"

"Six months, off and on."

"After another six months you'll know why it can't go on."

"I don't know; it suits me all right," said the man on the other side of Martin, a man with a jovial red rabbit-like face. "Of course, I don't like being dirty and smelling and all that, but one gets accustomed to it."

"But you are an Alsatian; you don't care."

"I was a baker. They're going to send me to Dijon soon to bake army bread. It'll be a change. There'll be wine and lots of little girls. Good God, how drunk I'll be; and, old chap, you just watch me with the women. . . ."

"I should just like to get home and not be ordered about," said the first man. "I've been lucky, though," he went on; "I've been kept most of the time in reserve. I only had to use my bayonet once."

"When was that?" asked Martin.

"Near Mont Cornélien, last year. We put them to the

bayonet and I was running and a man threw his arms up just in front of me saying, 'Mon ami, mon ami,' in French. I ran on because I couldn't stop, and I heard my bayonet grind as it went through his chest. I tripped over something and fell down."

"You were scared," said the Alsatian.

"Of course I was scared. I was trembling all over like an old dog in a thunderstorm. When I got up, he was lying on his side with his mouth open and blood running out, my bayonet still sticking into him. You know you have to put your foot against a man and pull hard to get the bayonet out."

"And if you're good at it," cried the Alsatian, "you ought to yank it out as your Boche falls and be ready for the next one. The time they gave me the Croix de Guerre I got three in succession, just like at drill."

"Oh, I was so sorry I had killed him," went on the other Frenchman. "When I went through his pockets I found a post-card. Here it is; I have it." He pulled out a cracked and worn leather wallet, from which he took a photograph and a bunch of pictures. "Look, this photograph was there, too. It hurt my heart. You see, it's a woman and two little girls. They look so nice. . . . It's strange, but I have two children, too, only one's a boy. I lay down on the ground beside him—I was all in—and listened to the machine-guns tapping put, put, put, put, put, all round. I wished I'd let him kill me instead. That was funny, wasn't it?"

"It's idiotic to feel like that. Put them to the bayonet,

all of them, the dirty Boches. Why, the only money I've had since the war began, except my five sous, was fifty francs I found on a German officer. I wonder where he got it, the old corpse-stripper."

"Oh, it's shameful! I am ashamed of being a man. Oh, the shame, the shame . . ." The other man buried his face in his hands.

"I wish they were serving out gniolle for an attack right now," said the Alsatian, "or the gniolle without the attack'd be better yet."

"Wait here," said Martin, "I'll go round to the copé and get a bottle of fizzy. We'll drink to peace or war, as you like. Damn this rain!"

"It's a shame to bury those boots," said the sergeant of the stretcher-bearers.

From the long roll of blanket on the ground beside the hastily-dug grave protruded a pair of high boots, new and well polished as if for parade. All about the earth was scarred with turned clay like raw wounds, and the tilting arms of little wooden crosses huddled together, with here and there a bent wreath or a faded bunch of flowers.

Overhead in the stripped trees a bird was singing.

"Shall we take them off? It's a shame to bury a pair of boots like that."

"So many poor devils need boots."

"Boots cost so dear."

Already two men were lowering the long bundle into the grave.

"Wait a minute; we've got a coffin for him."

A white board coffin was brought.

The boots thumped against the bottom as they put the big bundle in.

An officer strode into the enclosure of the graveyard, flicking his knees with a twig.

"Is this Lieutenant Dupont?" he asked of the sergeant.

"Yes, my lieutenant."

"Can you see his face?" The officer stooped and pulled apart the blanket where the head was.

"Poor René," he said. "Thank you. Good-bye," and strode out of the graveyard.

The yellowish clay fell in clots on the boards of the coffin. The sergeant bared his head and the aumonier came up, opening his book with a vaguely professional air.

"It was a shame to bury those boots. Boots are so dear nowadays," said the sergeant, mumbling to himself as he walked back towards the little broad shanty they used as a morgue.

Of the house, a little pale salmon-coloured villa, only a shell remained, but the garden was quite untouched; fall roses and bunches of white and pink and violet phlox bloomed there among the long grass and the intruding nettles. In the centre the round concrete fountain was no longer full of water, but a few brownish-green toads still inhabited it. The place smelt of box and sweetbriar and yew, and when you lay down on the grass where it grew short under the old yew tree by the fountain, you could see nothing but placid sky and waving green leaves. Martin Howe and Tom Randolph would spend there the quiet afternoons when they were off duty, sleeping in the languid sunlight, or chatting lazily, pointing out to each other tiny things, the pattern of snail-shells, the glitter of insects' wings, colours, fragrances that made vivid for them suddenly beauty and life, all that the shells that shrieked overhead, to explode on the road behind them, threatened to wipe out.

One afternoon Russell joined them, a tall young man with thin face and aquiline nose and unexpectedly light hair.

"Chef says we may go en repos in three days," he said, throwing himself on the ground beside the other two.

"We've heard that before," said Tom Randolph. "Division hasn't started out yet, ole boy; an' we're the last of the division."

"God, I'll be glad to go. . . . I'm dead," said Russell. "I was up all last night with dysentery."

"So was I. . . . It was not funny; first it'd be vomiting, and then diarrhœa, and then the shells'd start coming in. Gave me a merry time of it."

"They say it's the gas," said Martin.

"God, the gas! Turns me sick to think of it," said Russell, stroking his forehead with his hand. "Did I tell you about what happened to me the night after the attack, up in the woods?"

"No."

"Well, I was bringing a load of wounded down from P.J. right and I'd got just beyond the corner where the little muddy hill is—you know, where they're always shelling—when I found the road blocked. It was so God-damned black you couldn't see your hand in front of you. A camion'd gone off the road and another had run into it, and everything was littered with boxes of shells spilt about."

"Must have been real nice," said Randolph.

"The devilish part of it was that I was all alone. Coney was too sick with diarrhœa to be any use, so I left him up at the post, running out at both ends like he'd die. Well . . . I yelled and shouted like hell in my bad French and blew my whistle and sweated, and the damned wounded inside moaned and groaned. And the shells were coming in so thick I thought my number'd turn up any time. An' I couldn't get anybody. So I just climbed up in the second camion and backed it off into the bushes. . . . God, I bet it'll take a wrecking crew to get it out. . . .

"That was one good job.

"But there I was with another square in the road and no chance to pass that I could see in that darkness. Then what I was going to tell you about happened. I saw a little bit of light in a ditch beside a big car that seemed to be laying on its side, and I went down to it and there was a bunch of camion drivers, sitting round a lantern drinking.

" 'Hello, have a drink!' they called out to me, and one of them got up, waving his arms, ravin' drunk, and threw his arms around me and kissed me on the mouth. His hair and beard were full of wet mud. . . . Then he dragged me into the crowd.

" 'Ha, here's a copain come to die with us,' he cried.

"I gave him a shove and he fell down. But another one got up and handed me a tin cup full of that God-damned gniolle, that I drank not to make 'em sore. Then they all shouted, and stood about me, sayin', 'American's goin' to die with us. He's goin' to drink with us. He's goin' to die with us.' And the shells comin' in all the while. God, I was scared.

" 'I want to get a camion moved to the side of the road. . . . Good-bye,' I said. There didn't seem any use talkin' to them.

" 'But you've come to stay with us,' they said, and made me drink some more booze. 'You've come to die with us. Remember you said so.'

"The sweat was running into my eyes so's I could hardly see. I told 'em I'd be right back and slipped away into the dark. Then I thought I'd never get the second camion cranked. At last I managed it and put it so I could squeeze past, but they saw me and jumped up on the running-board of the ambulance, tried to stop the car, all yellin' at once, 'It's no use, the road's blocked both ways. You can't pass. You'd better stay and die with us. Caput.'

"Well, I put my foot on the accelerator and hit one of them so hard with the mud-guard he fell into the lantern and put it out. Then I got away. An' how I got past the stuff in that road afterwards was just luck. I couldn't see a God-damn thing; it was so black and I was so nerved up. God, I'll never forget these chaps' shoutin', 'Here's a feller come to die with us.' "

"Whew! That's some story," said Randolph.

"That'll make a letter home, won't it?" said Russell, smiling. "Guess my girl'll think I'm heroic enough after that."

Martin's eyes were watching a big dragonfly with brown body and cream and rainbow wings that hovered over the empty fountain and the three boys stretched on the grass, and was gone against the azure sky.

The prisoner had grey flesh, so grimed with mud that you could not tell if he were young or old. His uniform hung in a formless clot of mud about a slender frame. They had treated him at the dressing-station for a gash in his upper arm, and he was being used to help the stretcher-bearers. Martin sat in the front seat of the ambulance, watching him listlessly as he walked down the rutted road under the torn shreds of camouflage that fluttered a little in the wind. Martin wondered what he was thinking. Did he accept all this stench and filth and degradation of slavery as part of the divine order of things? Or did he too burn with loathing and revolt?

And all those men beyond the hill and the wood, what were they thinking? But how could they think? The lies they were drunk on would keep them eternally from thinking. They had never had any chance to think until they were hurried into the jaws of it, where was no room but for laughter and misery and the smell of blood.

The rutted road was empty now. Most of the batteries were quiet. Overhead in the brilliant sky aeroplanes snored monotonously.

The woods all about him were a vast rubbish-heap; the jagged, splintered boles of leafless trees rose in every direction from heaps of brass shell-cases, of tin cans, of bits of uniform and equipment. The wind came in puffs laden with an odour as of dead rats in an attic. And this was what all the centuries of civilisation had struggled for. For this had generations worn away their lives in mines and factories and forges, in fields and work-shops, toiling, screwing higher and higher the tension of their minds and muscles, polishing brighter and brighter the mirror of their intelligence. For this!

The German prisoner and another man had appeared in the road again, carrying a stretcher between them, walking with the slow, meticulous steps of great fatigue. A series of shells came in, like three cracks of a whip along the road. Martin followed the stretcher-bearers into the dugout.

The prisoner wiped the sweat from his grime-streaked forehead, and started up the step of the dugout again, a closed stretcher on his shoulder. Something made Martin look after him as he strolled down the rutted road. He wished he knew German so that he might call after the man and ask him what manner of a man he was.

Again, like snapping of a whip, three shells flashed yellow as they exploded in the brilliant sunlight of the road. The slender figure of the prisoner bent suddenly double, like a pocket-knife closing, and lay still. Martin ran out, stumbling in the hard ruts. In a soft child's voice the prisoner was babbling endlessly, contentedly. Martin kneeled beside him and tried to lift him, clasping him round the chest under the arms. He was very hard to lift, for his legs dragged limply in their soaked trousers, where the blood was beginning to saturate the muddy cloth, stickily. Sweat dripped from Martin's face, on the man's face, and he felt the arm-muscles and the ribs pressed against his body as he clutched the wounded man tightly to him in the effort of carrying him towards the dugout. The effort gave Martin a strange contentment. It was as if his body were taking part in the agony of this man's body. At last they were washed out, all the hatreds, all the lies, in blood and sweat. Nothing was left but the quiet friendliness of beings alike in every part, eternally alike.

Two men with a stretcher came from the dugout, and Martin laid the man's body, fast growing limper, less animated, down very carefully.

As he stood by the car, wiping the blood off his hands with an oily rag, he could still feel the man's ribs and the muscles of the man's arm against his side. It made him strangely happy.

At the end of the dugout a man was drawing short, hard breath as if he'd been running. There was the accustomed smell of blood and chloride and bandages and filthy miserable flesh. Howe lay on a stretcher wrapped in his blanket, with his coat over him, trying to sleep. There was very little light from a smoky lamp down at the end where the wounded were. The French batteries were fairly quiet, but the German shells were combing through the woods, coming in series of three and four, gradually nearing the dugout and edging away again. Howe saw the woods as a gambling table on which, throw after throw, scattered the random dice of death.

He pulled his blanket up round his head. He must sleep. How silly to think about it. It was luck. If a shell had his number on it he'd be gone before the words were out of his mouth. How silly that he might be dead any minute! What right had a nasty little piece of tinware to go tearing through his rich, feeling flesh, extinguishing it?

Like the sound of a mosquito in his ear, only louder, more vicious, a shell-shriek shrilled to the crash.

Damn! How foolish, how supremely silly that tired men somewhere away in the woods the other side of the lines should be shoving a shell into the breach of a gun to kill him, Martin Howe!

Like dice thrown on a table, shells burst about the dugout, now one side, now the other.

"Seem to have taken a fancy to us this evenin'," Howe heard Tom Randolph's voice from the bunk opposite.

"One," muttered Martin to himself, as he lay frozen with fear, flat on his back, biting his trembling lips, "two. . . . God, that was near!"

A dragging instant of suspense, and the shriek growing loud out of the distance.

"This is us." He clutched the sides of the stretcher.

A snorting roar rocked the dugout. Dirt fell in his

face. He looked about, dazed. The lamp was still burning. One of the wounded men, with a bandage like an
Arab's turban about his head, sat up in his stretcher with
wide, terrified eyes.

"God watches over drunkards and the feeble-minded.
Don't let's worry, Howe," shouted Randolph from his
bunk.

"That probably bitched car No. 4 for evermore," he
answered, turning on his stretcher, relieved for some
reason from the icy suspense.

"We should worry! We'll foot it home, that's all."

The casting of the dice began again, farther away this
time.

"We won that throw," thought Martin to himself.

Chapter VIII

DUCKS quacking woke Martin. For a moment he could not think where he was; then he remembered. The rafters of the loft of the farmhouse over his head were hung with bunches of herbs drying. He lay a long while on his back looking at them, sniffing the sweetened air, while farmyard sounds occupied his ears, hens cackling, the grunting of pigs, the rou-cou-cou-cou, rou-cou-cou-cou of pigeons under the eaves. He stretched himself and looked about him. He was alone except for Tom Randolph, who slept in a pile of blankets next to the wall, his head, with its close-cropped black hair, pillowed on his bare arm. Martin slipped off the canvas cot he had slept on and went to the window of the loft, a little square open at the level of the floor, through which came a dazzle of blue and gold and green. He looked out. Stables and hay-barns filled two sides of the farmyard below him. Behind them was a mass of rustling oak-trees. On the lichen-greened tile roofs pigeons strutted about, putting their coral feet daintily one before the other, puffing out their glittering breasts. He breathed deep of the smell of hay and manure and cows and of unpolluted farms.

From the yard came a riotous cackling of chickens and quacking of ducks, mingled with the peeping of the little broods. In the middle a girl in blue gingham, sleeves rolled up as far as possible on her brown arms, a girl with a mass of dark hair loosely coiled above the nape of her neck, was throwing to the fowls handfuls of grain with a wide gesture.

"And to think that only yesterday . . ." said Martin to himself. He listened carefully for some time. "Wonderful! You can't even hear the guns."

Chapter IX

THE evening was pearl-grey when they left the village; in their nostrils was the smell of the leisurely death of the year, of leaves drying and falling, of ripened fruit and bursting seed-pods.

"The fall's a maddening sort o' time for me," said Tom Randolph. "It makes me itch to get up on ma hind legs an' do things, go places."

"I suppose it's that the earth has such a feel of accomplishment," said Howe.

"You do feel as if Nature had pulled off her part of the job and was restin'."

They stopped a second and looked about them, breathing deep. On one side of the road were woods where in long alleys the mists deepened into purple darkness.

"There's the moon."

"God! it looks like a pumpkin."

"I wish those guns'd shut up 'way off there to the north."

"They're sort of irrelevant, aren't they?"

They walked on, silent, listening to the guns throbbing far away, like muffled drums beaten in nervous haste.

"Sounds almost like a barrage."

Martin for some reason was thinking of the last verses of Shelley's *Hellas*. He wished he knew them so that he could recite them.

> *"Faiths and empires gleam*
> *Like wrecks in a dissolving dream."*

The purple trunks of saplings passed slowly across the broad face of the moon as they walked along. How beautiful the world was!

"Look, Tom." Martin put his arm about Randolph's shoulder and nodded towards the moon. "It might be a ship with puffed-out pumpkin-coloured sails, the way the trees make it look now."

"Wouldn't it be great to go to sea?" said Randolph, looking straight into the moon, "an' get out of this slaughter-house. It's nice to see the war, but I have no intention of taking up butchery as a profession. . . . There is too much else to do in the world."

They walked slowly along the road talking of the sea, and Martin told how when he was a little kid he'd had an uncle who used to tell him about the Vikings and the Swan Path, and how one of the great moments of his life had been when he and a friend had looked out of their window in a little inn on Cape Cod one morning and seen the sea and the swaying gold path of the sun on it, stretching away, beyond the horizon.

"Poor old life," he said. "I'd expected to do so much with you." And they both laughed, a little bitterly.

They were strolling past a large farmhouse that stood like a hen among chicks in a crowd of little outbuildings. A man in the road lit a cigarette and Martin recognised him in the orange glare of the match.

"Monsieur Merrier!" He held out his hand. It was the aspirant he had drunk beer with weeks ago at Brocourt.

"Hah! It's you!"

"So you are en repos here, too?"

"Yes, indeed. But you two come in and see us; we are dying of the blues."

"We'd love to stop in for a second."

A fire smouldered in the big hearth of the farmhouse kitchen, sending a little irregular fringe of red light out over the tiled floor. At the end of the room towards the door three men were seated round a table, smoking. A candle threw their huge and grotesque shadows on the floor and on the whitewashed walls, and lit up the dark beams of that part of the ceiling. The three men got up and everyone shook hands, filling the room with swaying giant shadows. Champagne was brought and tin cups and more candles, and the Americans were given the two most comfortable chairs.

"It's such a find to have Americans who speak French," said a bearded man with unusually large brilliant eyes. He had been introduced as André Dubois, "a very terrible person," had added Merrier, laughing. The cork popped out of the bottle he had been struggling with.

"You see, we never can find out what you think about things. . . . All we can do is to be sympathetically inane, and *vive les braves alliés* and that sort of stuff."

"I doubt if we Americans do think," said Martin.

"Cigarettes, who wants some cigarettes?" cried Lully, a small man with a very brown oval face to which long eyelashes and a little bit of silky black moustache gave almost a winsomeness. When he laughed he showed brilliant, very regular teeth. As he handed the cigarettes about he looked searchingly at Martin with eyes disconcertingly intense. "Merrier has told us about you," he said. "You seem to be the first American we'd met who agreed with us."

"What about?"

"About the war, of course."

"Yes," took up the fourth man, a blonde Norman with an impressive, rather majestic face, "we were very interested. You see, we bore each other, talking always among ourselves. . . . I hope you won't be offended if I agree with you in saying that Americans never think. I've been in Texas, you see."

"Really?"

"Yes, I went to a Jesuit College in Dallas. I was preparing to enter the Society of Jesus."

"How long have you been in the war?" asked André Dubois, passing his hand across his beard.

"We've both been in the same length of time—about six months."

"Do you like it?"

"I don't have a bad time. . . . But the people in Boccaccio managed to enjoy themselves while the plague was at Florence. That seems to me the only way to take the war."

"We have no villa to take refuge in, though," said Dubois, "and we have forgotten all our amusing stories."

"And in America—they like the war?"

"They don't know what it is. They are like children. They believe everything they are told, you see; they have had no experience in international affairs, like you Europeans. To me our entrance into the war is a tragedy."

"It's sort of goin' back on our only excuse for existing," put in Randolph.

"In exchange for all the quiet and the civilisation and the beauty of ordered lives that Europeans gave up in going to the new world we gave them opportunity to earn luxury, and, infinitely more important, freedom from the past, that gangrened ghost of the past that is killing Europe to-day with its infection of hate and greed of murder.

"America has turned traitor to all that, you see; that's the way we look at it. Now we're a military nation, an organised pirate like France and England and Germany."

"But American idealism? The speeches, the notes?" cried Lully, catching the edge of the table with his two brown hands.

"Camouflage," said Martin.

"You mean it's insincere?"

"The best camouflage is always sincere."

Dubois ran his hands through his hair.

"Of course, why should there be any difference?" he said.

"Oh, we're all dupes, we're all dupes. Look, Lully, old man, fill up the Americans' glasses."

"Thanks."

"And I used to believe in liberty," said Martin. He raised his tumbler and looked at the candle through the pale yellow champagne. On the wall behind him, his arm and hand and the tumbler were shadowed huge in dusky lavender blue. He noticed that his was the only tumbler.

"I am honoured," he said; "mine is the only glass."

"And that's looted," said Merrier.

"It's funny . . ." Martin suddenly felt himself filled with a desire to talk. "All my life I've struggled for my own liberty in my small way. Now I hardly know if the thing exists."

"Exists? Of course it does, or people wouldn't hate it so," cried Lully.

"I used to think," went on Martin, "that it was my family I must escape from to be free; I mean all the conventional ties, the worship of success and the respectabilities that is drummed into you when you're young."

"I suppose everyone has thought that. . . ."

"How stupid we were before the war, how we prated of small revolts, how we sniggered over little jokes at religion and government. And all the while, in the infinite greed, in the infinite stupidity of men, this was being prepared." André Dubois was speaking, puffing nervously at a cigarette between phrases, now and then pulling at his beard with a long, sinewy hand.

"What terrifies me rather is their power to enslave our minds," Martin went on, his voice growing louder and surer as his idea carried him along. "I shall never forget the flags, the menacing, exultant flags along all the streets before we went to war, the gradual unbaring of teeth, gradual lulling to sleep of people's humanity and sense by the phrases, the phrases. . . . America, as you know, is ruled by the press. And the press is ruled by whom? Who shall ever know what dark forces bought and bought until we should be ready to go blinded and gagged to war? . . . People seem to so love to be fooled. Intellect used to mean freedom, a light struggling against darkness. Now the darkness is using the light for its own purposes. . . . We are slaves of bought intellect, willing slaves."

"But, Howe, the minute you see that and laugh at it,

you're not a slave. Laugh and be individually as decent as you can, and don't worry your head about the rest of the world; and have a good time in spite of the God-damned scoundrels," broke out Randolph in English. "No use worrying yourself into the grave over a thing you can't help."

"There is one solution and one only, my friends," said the blonde Norman; "the Church. . . ." He sat up straight in his chair, speaking slowly with expressionless face. "People are too weak and too kindly to shift for themselves. Government of some sort there must be. Lay Government has proved through all the tragic years of history to be merely a ruse of the strong to oppress the weak, of the wicked to fool the confiding. There remains only religion. In the organisation of religion lies the natural and suitable arrangement for the happiness of man. The Church will govern not through physical force but through spiritual force."

"The force of fear." Lully jumped to his feet impatiently, making the bottles sway on the table.

"The force of love. . . . I once thought as you do, my friend," said the Norman, pulling Lully back into his chair with a smile.

Lully drank a glass of champagne greedily and undid the buttons of his blue jacket.

"Go on," he said; "it's madness."

"All the evil of the Church," went on the Norman's even voice, "comes from her struggles to attain supremacy. Once assured of triumph, established as the rule of the world, it becomes the natural channel through which the wise rule and direct the stupid, not for their own interest, not for ambition for worldly things, but for the love that is in them. The freedom the Church offers is the only true freedom. It denies the world, and the slaveries and rewards of it. It gives the love of God as the only aim of life."

"But think of the Church to-day, the cardinals at Rome, the Church turned everywhere to the worship of tribal gods. . . ."

"Yes, but admit that that can be changed. The Church has been supreme in the past; can it not again be supreme? All the evil comes from the struggle, from the compromise. Picture to yourself for a moment a world conquered by the Church, ruled through the soul and mind, where force will not exist, where instead of all the multitudinous tyrannies man has choked his life with in organising against other men, will exist the one supreme thing, the Church of God. Instead of many hatreds, one love. Instead of many slaveries, one freedom."

"A single tyranny, instead of a million. What's the choice?" cried Lully.

"But you are both violent, my children." Merrier got to his feet and smilingly filled the glasses all round. "You go at the matter too much from the heroic point of view. All this sermonising does no good. We are very simple people who want to live quietly and have plenty to eat and have no one worry us or hurt us in the little span of sunlight before we die. All we have now is the same war between the classes: those that exploit and those that are exploited. The cunning, unscrupulous people control the humane, kindly people. This war that has smashed our little European world in which order was so painfully taking the place of chaos, seems to me merely a gigantic battle fought over the plunder of the world by the pirates who have grown fat to the point of madness on the work of their own people, on the work of the millions in Africa, in India, in America, who have come directly or indirectly under the yoke of the insane greed of the white races. Well, our edifice is ruined. Let's think no more of it. Ours is now the duty of rebuilding, reorganising. I have not faith enough in human nature to be an anarchist. . . . We are too like sheep; we must go in flocks, and a flock to live must organise. There is plenty for everyone, even with the huge growth in population all over the world. What we want is organisation from the bottom, organisation by the ungreedy, by the humane, by the uncunning, social-ism of the masses that shall spring from the natural need of men to help one another; not socialism from the top to the ends of the governors, that they may clamp us tighter in their fetters. We must stop the economic war, the war for existence of man against man. That will be the first step in the long climb to civilisation. They must co-operate, they must learn that it is saner and more advantageous to help one another than to hinder one another in the great war against nature. And the tyranny of the feudal money lords, the unspeakable misery of this war is driving men closer together into fraternity, co-operation. It is the lower classes, therefore, that the new world must be founded on. The rich must be extinguished; with them wars will die. First between rich and poor, between the exploiter and the exploited. . . ."

"They have one thing in common," interrupted the blonde Norman, smiling.

"What's that?"

"Humanity. . . . That is, feebleness, cowardice."

"No, indeed. All through the world's history there has been one law for the lord and another for the slave, one humanity for the lord and another humanity for the slave. What we must strive for is a true universal humanity."

"True," cried Lully, "but why take the longest, the most difficult road? You say that people are sheep; they must be driven. I say that you and I and our American friends here are not sheep. We are capable of standing alone, of judging all for ourselves, and we are just ordinary people like anyone else."

"Oh, but look at us, Lully!" interrupted Merrier. "We are too weak and too cowardly . . ."

"An example," said Martin, excitedly leaning across

the table. "We none of us believe that war is right or useful or anything but a hideous method of mutual suicide. Have we the courage of our own faith?"

"As I said," Merrier took up again, "I have too little faith to be an anarchist, but I have too much to believe in religion." His tin cup rapped sharply on the table as he set it down.

"No," Lully continued, after a pause, "it is better for man to worship God, His image on the clouds, the creation of his fancy, than to worship the vulgar apparatus of organised life, government. Better sacrifice his children to Moloch than to that society for the propagation and protection of commerce, the nation. Oh, think of the cost of government in all the ages since men stopped living in marauding tribes! Think of the great men martyred. Think of the thought trodden into the dust. . . . Give man a chance for once. Government should be purely utilitarian, like the electric light wires in a house. It is a method for attaining peace and comfort —a bad one, I think, at that; not a thing to be worshipped as God. The one reason for it is the protection of property. Why should we have property? That is the central evil of the world. . . . That is the cancer that has made life a hell of misery until now; the inflated greed of it has spurred on our nations of the West to throw themselves back, for ever, perhaps, into the depths of savagery. . . . Oh, if people would only trust their own

fundamental kindliness, the fraternity, the love that is
the strongest thing in life. Abolish property, and the
disease of the desire for it, the desire to grasp and have,
and you'll need no government to protect you. The
vividness and resiliency of the life of man is being fast
crushed under organisation, tabulation. Overorganisa-
tion is death. It is disorganisation, not organisation, that
is the aim of life."

"I grant that what all of you say is true, but why say
it over and over again?" André Dubois talked, striding
back and forth beside the table, his arms gesticulating.
His compound shadow thrown by the candles on the
white wall followed him back and forth, mocking him
with huge blurred gestures. "The Greek philosophers
said it and the Indian sages. Our descendants thousands
of years from now will say it and wring their hands as
we do. Has not someone on earth the courage to
act? . . ." The men at the table turned towards him,
watching his tall figure move back and forth.

"We are slaves. We are blind. We are deaf. Why
should we argue, we who have no experience of different things to go on? It has always been the same: man
the slave of property or religion, of his own shadow.
. . . First we must burst our bonds, open our eyes,
clear our ears. Now we know nothing but what we are
told by the rulers. Oh, the lies, the lies, the lies, the lies
that life is smothered in! We must strike once more for

freedom, for the sake of the dignity of man. Hopelessly, cynically, ruthlessly we must rise and show at least that we are not taken in; that we are slaves but not willing slaves. Oh, they have deceived us so many times. We have been such dupes, we have been such dupes!"

"You are right," said the blonde Norman sullenly; "we have all been dupes."

A sudden self-consciousness chilled them all to silence for a while. Without wanting to, they strained their ears to hear the guns. There they were, throbbing loud, unceasing, towards the north, like hasty muffled drumbeating.

> *"Cease; drain not to its dregs the wine,*
> *Of bitter Prophecy.*
> *The world is weary of its past.*
> *Oh, might it die or rest at last."*

All through the talk snatches from *Hellas* had been running through Howe's head.

After a long pause he turned to Merrier and asked him how he had fared in the attack.

"Oh, not so badly. I brought my skin back," said Merrier, laughing. "It was a dull business. After waiting eight hours under gas bombardment we got orders to advance, and so over we went with the barrage way ahead of us. There was no resistance where we were. We took a lot of prisoners and blew up some dugouts and I had the good luck to find a lot of German choco-

late. It came in handy, I can tell you, as no ravitaillement came for two days. We just had biscuits and I
toasted the biscuits and chocolate together and had
quite good meals, though I nearly died of thirst afterwards. . . . We lost heavily, though, when they started
counterattacking."

"An' no one of you were touched?"

"Luck. . . . But we lost many dear friends. Oh, it's
always like that."

"Look what I brought back—a German gun," said
André Dubois, going to the corner of the room.

"That's some souvenir," said Tom Randolph, sitting
up suddenly, shaking himself out of the reverie he had
been sunk in all through the talk of the evening.

"And I have three hundred rounds. They'll come in
handy some day."

"When?"

"In the revolution—after the war."

"That's the stuff I like to hear," cried Randolph, getting to his feet. "Why wait for the war to end?"

"Why? Because we have not the courage. . . . But it
is impossible until after the war."

"And then you think it is possible?"

"Yes."

"Will it accomplish anything?"

"God knows."

"One last bottle of champagne," cried Merrier.

They seated themselves round the table again. Martin

took in at a glance the eager sunburned faces, the eyes burning with hope, with determination, and a sudden joy flared through him.

"Oh, there is hope," he said, drinking down his glass. "We are too young, too needed to fail. We must find a way, find the first step of a way to freedom, or life is a hollow mockery."

"To Revolution, to Anarchy, to the Socialist state," they all cried, drinking down the last of the champagne. All the candles but one had guttered out. Their shadows swayed and darted in long arms and changing, grotesque limbs about the room.

"But first there must be peace," said the Norman, Jean Chenier, twisting his mouth into a faintly bitter smile.

"Oh, indeed, there must be peace."

"Of all slaveries, the slavery of war, of armies, is the bitterest, the most hopeless slavery." Lully was speaking, his smooth brown face in a grimace of excitement and loathing. "War is our first enemy."

"But oh, my friend," said Merrier, "we will win in the end. All the people in all the armies of the world believe as we do. In all the minds the seed is sprouting."

"Before long the day will come. The tocsin will ring."

"Do you really believe that?" cried Martin. "Have we the courage, have we the energy, have we the power? Are we the men our ancestors were?"

"No," said Dubois, crashing down on the table with his fist; "we are merely intellectuals. We cling to a mummified world. But they have the power and the nerve."

"Who?"

"The stupid average working-people."

"We only can combat the lies," said Lully; "they are so easily duped. After the war that is what we must do."

"Oh, but we are all such dupes," cried Dubois. "First we must fight the lies. It is the lies that choke us."

It was very late. Howe and Tom Randolph were walking home under a cold white moon already well sunk in the west; northward was a little flickering glare above the tops of the low hills and a sound of firing as of muffled drums beaten hastily.

"With people like that we needn't despair of civilisation," said Howe.

"With people who are young and aren't scared you can do lots."

"We must come over and see those fellows again. It's such a relief to be able to talk."

"And they give you the idea that something's really going on in the world, don't they?"

"Oh, it's wonderful! Think that the awakening may come soon."

"We might wake up to-morrow and . . ."

"It's too important to joke about; don't be an ass, Tom."

They rolled up in their blankets in the silent barn and listened to the drum-fire in the distance. Martin saw again, as he lay on his side with his eyes closed, the group of men in blue uniforms, men with eager brown faces and eyes gleaming with hope, and saw their full red lips moving as they talked.

The candle threw the shadows of their heads, huge, fantastic, and of their gesticulating arms on the white walls of the kitchen. And it seemed to Martin Howe that all his friends were gathered in that room.

Chapter X

"THEY say you sell shoe-laces," said Martin, his eyes blinking in the faint candlelight.

Crouched in the end of the dugout was a man with a brown skin like wrinkled leather, and white eyebrows and moustaches. All about him were piles of old boots, rotten with wear and mud, holding fantastically the imprints of the toes and ankle-bones of the feet that had worn them. The candle cast flitting shadows over them so that they seemed to move back and forth faintly, as do the feet of wounded men laid out on the floor of the dressing-station.

"I'm a cobbler by profession," said the man. He made a gesture with the blade of his knife in the direction of a huge bundle of leather laces that hung from a beam above his head. "I've done all those since yesterday. I cut up old boots into laces."

"Helps out the five sous a bit," said Martin, laughing.

"This post is convenient for my trade," went on the cobbler, as he picked out another boot to be cut into laces, and started hacking the upper part off the worn sole. "At the little hut, where they pile up the stiffs before they bury them—you know, just to the left outside the abri—they leave lots of their boots around. I can pick up any number I want." With a clasp-knife he was cutting the leather in a spiral, paring off a thin lace. He contracted his bushy eyebrows as he bent over his work. The candlelight glinted on the knife blade as he twisted it about dexterously.

"Yes, many a good copain of mine has had his poor feet in those boots. What of it? Some day another fellow will be making laces out of mine, eh?" He gave a wheezy, coughing laugh.

"I guess I'll take a pair. How much are they?"

"Six sous."

"Good."

The coins glinted in the light of the candle as they clinked in the man's leather-blackened palm.

"Good-bye," said Martin. He walked past men sleeping in the bunks on either side as he went towards the steps.

At the end of the dugout the man crouched on his pile of old leather, with his knife that glinted in the candlelight dexterously carving laces out of the boots of those who no longer needed them.

Chapter XI

THERE is no sound in the poste de secours. A faint greenish light filters down from the quiet woods outside. Martin is kneeling beside a stretcher where lies a mass of torn blue uniform crossed in several places by strips of white bandages clotted with dark blood. The massive face, grimed with mud, is very waxy and grey. The light hair hangs in clots about the forehead. The nose is sharp, but there is a faint smile about the lips made thin by pain.

"Is there anything I can get you?" asks Martin softly.

"Nothing." Slowly the blue eyelids uncover hazel eyes that burn feverishly.

"But you haven't told me yet, how's Merrier?"

"A shell . . . dead . . . poor chap."

"And the anarchist, Lully?"

"Dead."

"And Dubois?"

"Why ask?" came the faint rustling voice peevishly. "Everybody's dead. You're dead, aren't you?"

"No, I'm alive, and you. A little courage. . . . We must be cheerful."

"It's not for long. To-morrow, the next day. . . ." The blue eyelids slip back over the crazy burning eyes and the face takes on again the waxen look of death.

Publisher's Note

THE complete story of the first edition of *One Man's Initiation: 1917* will probably never be known. The original manuscript and corrected page proofs have long since disappeared, as have publisher's records and correspondence between publisher and author. Memory must be relied upon to fill in the gaps, and memory is notoriously unreliable—particularly when the events in question occurred half a century ago. This much is clear, however: the book, John Dos Passos' first novel, was initially published in October 1920 by George Allen & Unwin Ltd., of London; in June 1922, the first American edition was issued by the George H. Doran Company, of New York. Allen & Unwin printed 1,250 sets of sheets, of which they bound 750; after the Allen & Unwin title page was canceled, the remaining 500 sheets were shipped to Doran, who tipped in their own title page and bound the books for publication in America.* Except for the title-page leaves, the contents of the two

---

* Jack Potter, *A Bibliography of John Dos Passos* (Chicago: Normandie House, 1950), pp. 15, 22.

editions were identical in every respect. Neither edition ever went into a second printing.

In 1945 the Philosophical Library reprinted the book under the title *First Encounter*. Although the text was reset, it was not altered. The present edition, therefore —for reasons set forth below—can properly be described as the first authentic, unexpurgated version of the novel ever published.

In April 1959 the Cornell University Library purchased, from the Seven Gables Bookshop in New York City, a set of uncorrected page proofs of the Allen & Unwin edition. (Seven Gables had bought the proofs from William J. McElwee of Philadelphia, but it was never learned how Mr. McElwee had acquired them.) When the proofs were compared with the published version, discrepancies were found. A number of passages in the proofs, largely of dialogue, appeared to have been softened and somewhat laundered. When first shown the proofs, Mr. Dos Passos could not explain the changes. Some years later, perhaps when he was doing research preparatory to writing his book of reminiscences, *The Best Times,* he became convinced that the changes had been made contrary to his wishes. He was then able to recall having been informed by Allen & Unwin that the printer had refused to proceed with the book unless some modifications were made in the dialogue. He finally agreed to the bowdlerization, but he does not recollect ever having seen or approved specific changes.

In 1967, when Robert H. Elias, Goldwin Smith Professor of English Literature at Cornell University, proposed that Cornell University Press publish the novel for the first time in the form in which it was originally written, Mr. Dos Passos readily consented. The publisher here wishes to express gratitude to Professor Elias for initiating the project and for helping to see it through to publication. Thanks are also due to the staff of the Cornell University Libraries for their helpful cooperation.

This edition was set from the original page proofs, after they were scrupulously read against a copy of the first edition. Because the proof contained a number of typographical errors and some errors and inconsistencies in capitalization and punctuation, approximately thirty lines in our edition were altered to conform to the first edition. Two examples of this sort of change should suffice: on the next-to-last line of page 44 of the proof, the word "letcherous" appears; it was corrected in the first edition and appears correctly spelled in our edition (p. 82, l. 11). On page 12, line 11, of the proof, the phrase "of the snap fingers" was corrected, in the first edition and in this edition (p. 46, l. 16), to "snap of the fingers."

In about a dozen places, the present edition differs from both the page proof and the first edition. On page 87, line 3, in both proof and book, a sentence begins "He went so see headquarters in that get-up"; the third word of the sentence has been changed to "to" in this edition (p. 129, l. 8). Similarly, two references to "hors d'oeuvre" (p. 50, l. 28; p. 51, l. 12, of proof and first edition) have been corrected to read "hors d'oeuvres" (p. 88, l. 27; p. 89, l. 15). No changes were, of course, made without the author's consent, and Mr. Dos Passos read and approved final proof.

The significant differences between this edition of the book and the first edition are as follows.

Page 53, lines 5–9. *The first edition (p. 18, l. 32–p. 19, l. 2) reads:*

"Gee, these Frenchwomen are immoral. They say the war does it."

"Can't be that. Nothing is more purifying than sacrifice."

"A feller has to be mighty careful, they say."

Page 73, lines 18–20. *The first edition (p. 37, ll. 3–5) reads:*

". . . Anyway, she comes up to me with a funny look in her eyes an' starts makin' love to me. . . ."

Page 75, lines 1–3. *In the first edition (p. 38) these lines were omitted entirely. Inserted between lines 4–5 of the present version was the line:*

"We are," they shouted.

Page 97, lines 18–19. *The words* " 'I'll sleep without a man' " *were changed, in the first edition* (*p. 59, l. 5*), *to* " 'I have not made a sou.' "

Page 98, line 15, to page 99, line 2. *The first edition* (*p. 59, l. 33–p. 60, l. 15*) *reads:*

They stopped under a broken sign of black letters on greyish glass, within which one feeble electric light bulb made a red glow. The pavement was wet, and glimmered where it slanted up to the lamp-post at the next corner.

"Here we are. Come along, Janey," cried the Australian in a brisk voice.

The door opened and slammed again. Martin and the other girl stood on the pavement facing each other. The Englishman collapsed on the doorstep, and began to snore.

"Well, there's only you and me," she said.

"Oh, if you were only a person, instead of being a member of a profession——" said Martin softly.

Page 111, lines 3–6. *The first edition* (*p. 71, ll. 24–27*) *reads:*

and asked the swaying figure in his mind:

"And You, what do You think of it?"

For an instant he could feel wire barbs ripping through his own flesh.